She was stealing his car!

"Hey, you!" Anger roiled through Mac's gut at the sheer audacity of the thief. A sexy *female* thief in the tightest, shortest pair of shorts he'd ever seen.

The woman leaned over between the tow truck and the Morgan, her backside in the air. Mac snapped his mouth shut and took in the stunning view while his mind blanked out.

Every boy's dream came to life before his eyes: a big truck and a pretty girl, all at once. He'd had a thing for Daisy Duke shorts, ever since watching the adventures of the original good ol' boys and their sexy cousin when he was ten.

But this was no rerun. This was here and now, and this woman was right in front of him, tilted so perfectly he could see the bottom of the fleshy mounds at the top of each leg, flesh that bloomed into a set of cheeks that sat high and round on the top of a great set of shapely feminine legs. Mac's blood rushed south of his waist and his mouth went dry. If he wasn't so anxious to figure out just what she was doing, he'd stand there a moment, simply enjoying the view.

And suddenly, he realized that's exactly what he'd been doing....

Blaze

Dear Reader,

It's such a thrill to be part of the Blaze series. The heat level of Blaze books suits my idea of a rocking good read every time.

Ideas for stories sometimes come to me in flashes. For *Possessing Morgan*, I had a visual of an exotic car dangling off the back of a rattletrap old tow truck. The truck and car bounced and groaned down a manicured driveway toward distant gates. That vision stayed with me for a couple of years. Whenever I saw that car and truck, I'd add pieces of the story.

Then, I had an idea for a secondary character who'd once been a car thief. Voila! I had the tow truck operator...except she's a red-haired spitfire in Daisy Duke shorts. After that, the story flew onto the keyboard and I had the essence of *Possessing Morgan*.

To be on the shelves with a Harlequin Blaze with my little quirky vision come to life is one of the biggest thrills of my career.

I would be tickled if you checked my Web site for sample chapters of my other works at www.bonnieedwards.com, and don't forget to check the Blaze authors' blog at http://blazeauthors.com/blog/ for contests and up-to-date news. I love to hear from readers, so don't be shy and say hi!

Thank you for allowing me to entertain you.

Bonnie Edwards

Bonnie Edwards

POSSESSING MORGAN

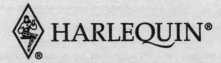

TORONTO • NEW YORK • LONDON
AMSTERDAM • PARIS • SYDNEY • HAMBURG
STOCKHOLM • ATHENS • TOKYO • MILAN • MADRID
PRAGUE • WARSAW • BUDAPEST • AUCKLAND

Recycling programs
for this product may
not exist in your area.

ISBN-13: 978-0-373-79533-8

POSSESSING MORGAN

ABOUT THE AUTHOR

Bonnie Edwards has sold everything from luxury bathroom fixtures to lingerie but loves writing sexy romances best. She lives on an island with her husband and a variety of pets within view of the Coast Mountains and the City of Vancouver. Bonnie enjoys teaching writing in continuing education classes at a local university.

In 2006, she helped launch the Kensington Aphrodisia erotic romance line.

She's thrilled to debut her Harlequin Blaze *Possessing Morgan* in March 2010. Bonnie loves to hear from readers! For excerpts and news please click on over to www.bonnieedwards.com.

Books by Bonnie Edwards
HARLEQUIN BLAZE
529—POSSESSING MORGAN

Don't miss any of our special offers. Write to us at the following address for information on our newest releases.

Harlequin Reader Service
U.S.: 3010 Walden Ave., P.O. Box 1325, Buffalo, NY 14269
Canadian: P.O. Box 609, Fort Erie, Ont. L2A 5X3

For my sisters:
Jaunice, the strongest woman I know
And Linda, one of the sweetest

1

A SPEAR OF LATE-AFTERNOON sun cleared a corner of the warehouse and cut through Morgan Swann's windshield. The alley's Dumpsters, discarded food wrappers and bottles disappeared in the sudden brilliance. She pulled the visor down to block the glare, then slipped on her sunglasses. As heat rose inside the truck cab, she rolled her window down a crack for ventilation, but only a crack. She couldn't afford to have someone reach in and drag her out.

"The last customer pulled away," she said as she started the ignition and Bessie rumbled to life.

Her lone passenger and partner on this gig sat up. Joe Calder slid his cap to the back of his head. He'd been dozing, face covered against the light.

"Showtime," he responded as he buckled his seat belt.

Morgan shifted Bessie into Drive and a familiar lust grew inside her as they moved forward. "I love stealing cars!"

"You've gotta stop thinking that way," Joe warned. "This is no time to get sloppy."

"Yak, yak, yak." She tapped her fingers and thumb

together to mime his mouth. "You sound like BB." The
office manager and Morgan's best friend. She braked,
then shifted into Reverse to guide the tow truck into the
far corner of the warehouse where the target sat, nose
out. The sunlight disappeared as they crawled backward
into the darkness. Joe reached over and removed her
sunglasses so her eyes could adjust.

"Guy in the office just perked up, Morgan. Move
it."

"Yee-hah!"

She cozied Bessie up to the front of the Charger they
were after, then leaped out with Joe and dropped the
T-bar to the floor. She glanced toward the glass-walled
office and sweat broke out all over her body. The man
inside reached low under his desk and came back up with
a tire iron in his hand.

"It seems he was expecting us," she said. Joe was
slower in getting the loops around the front tire on his
side, but their time was still excellent. In twenty seconds,
Morgan jumped back into Bessie's front seat.

Not a second too soon, either. The guy from the office moved quickly now, dodging around racks of home-
renovation materials. The look on his face took fury to
an all-new high.

"Get the hell in here!" she shouted, but Joe had already bounced into his seat. She slammed Bessie into
Drive and wished the old girl accelerated faster. Diesel
wasn't quick enough sometimes.

The doors to the loading bay just ahead geared up to
close. A sudden clang and clatter told her the tire iron
had hit Bessie's back end. "Poor baby." She patted the
dashboard and jammed her foot to the floor.

Joe reached for the radio and BB responded immediately. "Got the Charger?" her voice crackled.

"Yes."

"Any problems?" BB sounded suspicious.

As soon as Bessie broke free into the daylight, Morgan turned left and gunned her to get the car out, too.

"No problems," Joe said with a wink and a thumbs-up for Morgan. "ETA thirty minutes—I'm out," he told BB, cutting off any further questions.

Morgan checked the side mirror. The Charger's former owner had followed them into the alley. He stood in front of the now-closed bay doors, fists raised and mouth working. She heard curses a sailor might use. The end of the alley was ten feet ahead while the deadbeat was over a hundred feet behind.

Morgan rolled down her window and flipped him the bird. He responded with another furious toss of the tire iron.

Joe looked out the back window. "He needs anger management classes."

"He needs to pay his debts," she responded, then let out a rebel yell as she cleared the alley and hit the cross street.

Joe laughed. "You must've been a hell of a car thief."

"I was a *great* car thief." Sweet adrenaline pulsed and kicked her heart into high gear. "At least I thought so until the day I got caught."

Joe smirked. "Like most criminals you figured you could outrun the system?" He cast her a sidelong look.

"I was young enough to believe a smooth-talking jerk. If it hadn't been for a judge who intervened on my behalf, I'd have been up the brown creek without a paddle." She shuddered to think what might have happened if she'd maintained her connections to DeLongo's gang. A starstruck girl in desperate need of attention, she'd been far too easy to impress.

He gave her a curious glance. "Why are you telling me this?"

"The first time one of the drivers found out about my youthful indiscretions—" she chuckled at the phrase "—he tried to blackmail me." Which had been nothing to laugh at at the time. She'd been furious for trusting him with what she considered her secret shame. *To hell with that.*

"For money?" Joe blurted.

Clearly, he hadn't grasped the context of blackmail for *some* men. She cocked an eyebrow at him until his face went red and he swore under his breath.

"Not for money," he said, and shook his head.

"I learn from my mistakes. Since then, I've had this particular conversation with any of the guys who hang around longer than a few weeks. I'll never be put in a situation like that again." She hated being vulnerable, and keeping the secret of her criminal past had opened the door to harassment. It had been only one in a long string of life lessons.

With luck, she had learned everything she needed.

"Because of the help and support I got back in my teens, I've now got a great life," she admitted. "I couldn't ask for a job I'm better suited for. I love the hunt and chase, the occasional surprise during a pickup, and since repo is legal, I have the best of both worlds." The adrenaline junkie inside her needed a regular fix and this job provided it.

She thanked her lucky stars that she'd been smart enough to see the hard, dark road she'd stumbled down. Life had been damn fine ever since she'd been given a chance to take the right path. Her volunteer time at the youth center was her way of paying the judge's kindness forward.

A love life that gave her as much satisfaction as the other areas of her life still eluded her. A couple smooth-talking charmers had cured her of bad boys.

She hoped.

She wasn't sure she should test that theory and her hesitation kept her lonely. Not that she ever admitted to loneliness. With friends and coworkers Morgan culti-vated the image of happily single.

Joe lifted her clipboard off the dashboard to reveal her newest copy of the *World Courier.* She blanched. She didn't care if her partner found out she enjoyed the odd bit of sensational tabloid gossip. It was the top news story she didn't want Joe to notice. She'd misplaced the paper in her haste to follow up on BB's brilliant detective work tracking the Charger and she hadn't been able to read more than the headline.

But Joe, all business, read the work order on top and ignored the tabloid. "BB did a good job finding this guy." Admiration rang in his voice.

"You've got a thing for BB."

"She's a fine-looking woman under all that makeup." He watched the traffic from his side. "Nice features. Warm eyes."

"That was one of the longest speeches I've ever heard from you." He was more astute than she'd realized. "Most men don't notice her face." Or her soft, vulner-able eyes.

"Most men aren't me." The finality in his tone said the subject was closed.

Too bad. BB was her best friend and needed spe-cial care, so Morgan pushed. "She's been hurt more than once, Joe. She doesn't need a line of *BS*." Her tone was just as final. Mess with BB and you messed with Morgan, too.

"That's fine, I don't hand out *lines*."

She studied his hard-edged profile. "See that you don't." If she were a man, Joe's comments might be different. He might point out BB's natural double D's. Lush and round all over, BB had told Morgan she'd developed early. Morgan suspected her friend's full parade of makeup was more self-defense than enhancement of her pretty features.

Still, Joe's quiet confidence and thoughtful conversation stood out among the yahoos they had working the rigs. Joe had only been with Five Aces Towing a couple weeks. Maybe he was different. Maybe he did like BB for who she was rather than the size of her chest. Her friend was one of the warmest people Morgan had ever known. Fiercely loyal, BB cared too much about people. Even when they didn't care back.

Morgan could warn Joe about BB's decision to steer clear of the drivers, but maybe, just maybe, Joe was different enough to change BB's mind.

When they got to the office, she would let Joe go in ahead of her. She wanted to catch up on her reading about Kingston McRae. The memory of the headline she'd read earlier taunted her.

Wealthy playboy Kingston McRae returns from parts unknown after a mysterious and extended absence

She had an affinity for Kingston McRae and had missed the stories about him. The playboy tycoon had been out of sight for three months and twelve days. She felt parched for information.

An "affinity" was a new, more adult way to admit she had a secret, girly crush. The tabloid called to her and she itched to get to page two where the story continued. Maybe there'd be more pictures of the delicious Kingston McRae.

After they dropped the Charger off in the company's impound lot, she drove two blocks to the office.

A squat square building, the offices of Five Aces Towing looked like a circa 1940 gas station with scalloped overhang and two-bay garage. The company had been headquartered here since BB's uncle had started the business.

After an insecure childhood Morgan finally had the security she'd always wanted. She made decent money and loved the adrenaline that kept things just this side of reckless while the necessity of recovery kept her on the right side of legal.

At fifteen, she'd been charmed by Johnny DeLongo. A mistake she'd learned from. She could now spot a charmer a mile off. He had impressed her with fast cars, fancy restaurants and what her fifteen-year-old heart believed were declarations of devotion.

Hah! She'd been fooled. Somehow, Johnny had recognized that her love of fast cars could be turned to his advantage. Before she knew it she was on the fast track to prison, hooked on the rush that came with boosting cars. She was only glad she'd been caught while she was still a minor.

The moment she pulled into her parking spot, Joe jumped out and strode quickly for the door. She hadn't had to prod him to go inside without her, so she picked up her paper and settled into her seat. Kingston McRae, man about town, bachelor playboy and all-around hunk o' man, looked hot in every sense of the word. Tall,

commanding, in charge. The picture was clear and focused. The photographer must have been in the front
lines of the crowd at the movie premiere.

> *The pages of the* World Courier *have been bereft
> without the handsome McRae. Seen here with star-
> let Jakeera Sofia, McRae arrives at the premiere of
> her movie,* Teenage Terror, *Friday night. Informed
> sources say McRae and the lovely Jakeera are so
> hot for each other they had sex in the limo. Is
> that a smudge of DNA on her lip? This reporter's
> dying to know.*

The idea of being alone with him in the back of a limo
flushed her with arousal. Her panties moist, she took a
guilty glance around the lot. She was alone, so she took
another moment to skim the article.

She should get a grip on this girly nonsense, but since
fantasizing about him had helped save her from falling
back into a life of crime, it was hard to let him go.

Right now, life was great. All she lacked was a sex
life. Her Kingston fantasies were her only release.

Seven years ago, she'd been jobless, broke and down-
hearted, tired of the effort it took to stay on the straight
and narrow. Tempted to go back to car theft to make a
living, just in time, she'd stumbled across a picture of
Kingston McRae. The model on his arm had looked a
lot like Morgan: auburn-haired with a square face and
green eyes. Visualizing herself in a photo with McRae
had been the lifesaving technique she'd needed.

It had been easy to dream that his engaging, warm
smile was for her, that his feelings for her were true, ran
deep and strong. And if she could just hold on awhile
longer, better days were around the corner. Crushing

on Kingston McRae was her only flight of fancy, because life had taught her to take care of her own business and to depend on no one. Unlike her juvenile file, adult records were public and she seesawed about going back to a business that had been exciting but deadly dangerous. She let her dreams of McRae play out—dreams were safe—and put her energy into finding a good job in the real world.

A week after her fantasy life began with the playboy tycoon she found Five Aces. But once she learned answering phones wasn't as much fun as the hands-on recoveries, she'd badgered BB to let her go out on a job. The other drivers had laid bets she would cut and run when things got scary, but car theft was something she'd been good at, and the thrill of the chase made recovery a natural fit. She'd never gone back to the phones.

Page two of the story said that an informed source reported McRae had met this most recent starlet at a charity ball. There was speculation about marriage, but so far, McRae had avoided more engagements than any rich bachelor had a right to.

The man was prime, no doubt about it.

If she met him, just once, maybe she could let her fantasy go and open her heart to someone more in her league. After a night filled with dreams of him she woke overheated, the sheet twisted, her heart pounding. Her emotions were raw for the whole day as she struggled to tamp down her sexual nature.

She fought hard to keep her fantasy life separate from reality. Most of the time she won the battle, but lately her dreams had invaded her daytime thoughts.

The whole thing stemmed from hormones rather than loneliness, so she ignored her need most of the time. But she'd taken on more dangerous gigs, looking for another kind of outlet. It was definitely time to do something about the lack of sex before she went too far.

All she needed was to hook up for a night. Work out some of her frustrations. Up until a couple of weeks ago, BB had been a regular at a bar downtown. The two of them could have a girls' night out.

Spending quality time—realistic, adult, seductive time—under the sheets with a man could kick her fantasies of Kingston McRae to the curb.

If she found release with a man, she wouldn't need the rush of danger.

She wasn't hard on the eyes. Her trim butt and flat tummy looked pretty good in jeans. Her hair was thick and full. The color wasn't bad either. Men liked to touch her hair and tell her how soft it was.

She lifted her ball cap to smooth the top of her head. If Kingston ever had the chance, he'd run his long fingers through her hair. She pulled off the elastic band and threaded her hand through the warm strands. They separated and slipped through her sensitive fingers.

He'd sigh at the feel while his thumb brushed against her neck, then her ear lobe, before he leaned in close to nuzzle the delicate skin of her throat.

Her eyes drifted closed as she indulged herself with images of Kingston. These quiet musings often came on the heels of the rush she chased, connecting the adrenaline and sexual desire in a way she never wanted to give up. She reveled in the imagined croon of his voice, deep and hypnotic as he took her down into a world filled with sighs, need and dark arousal.

Her nipples beaded and she sensed the moisture between her thighs as desire seeped through her. She knew nothing about the physicality of the man—his scent, the feel of his hair, the warmth and texture of his skin. But no other man had roused these feelings in her.

The adrenaline rush subsided as sexual arousal pulsed warmly through her. She soaked it up until she couldn't delay any longer.

It was normal to walk around on a low sexual boil these days, so when she opened Bessie's door and jumped to the ground, she felt revved. She'd pick up batteries after work and tonight at home she'd finish what her fantasy had started. Alone.

It seemed the only guarantee of ending the night with a bang, as it were. She sighed.

The chances of a woman like her meeting Kingston McRae were nil, so it was time to grow up. She'd managed for over three months without news of the man, and just because he'd surfaced again was no reason to go back to the same silly behavior.

The fantasy must die!

She smoothed a hand over her belly and strode through the door into the office. Straight into a hotbed of emotion.

The atmosphere was so charged, Morgan slammed to a halt. She took in BB's face, then Joe's, their expressions taut with tension. She couldn't tell if it was sexual energy or anger, but it swirled hot and thick around them.

BB sat in the back of the office, away from the front counter. It was safer in case one of the disgruntled victims of a repo came in for a pound of flesh. Morgan suspected BB could handle herself in a scuffle, but thankfully, she'd never seen her friend tested.

Her arrival broke the tension and BB twirled her chair to face her desk again. But a telltale tremor in her hands told Morgan plenty.

While she'd been fantasizing about the delectable

Kingston McRae, Joe had been in here, tantalizing BB in his quiet, easygoing way.

Too bad Morgan had missed it.

Joe stood beside the coffee station, nonchalantly sipping out of his gigantic travel mug.

She let go of the idea of a girls' night out. If BB didn't see where this was headed with Joe, she was blind. And BB being blind to men was like—*well, that just wouldn't happen!*

"Next time I tell you to take back up," BB snapped at her, "don't argue." Obviously Joe had mentioned the tire iron.

Probably to get into BB's good books. Or her pants.

Morgan hadn't argued with the office manager about taking Joe along today, but it was safer not to remind her of that fact. BB made a great tracer because she often got gut feelings about which jobs could go screwy. The tire iron counted as screwy.

"Yes, ma'am," she replied. She hid a smirk as she flipped up the counter and walked over to Joe, who stood studying his boots. She needed coffee and to poke him in the ribs for tattling.

"Ma'am! I'm only two years older than you." BB swung around in her creaky oak chair, stiletto bobbling at the end of her crossed leg. She smoothed her T-shirt over her natural double D's and glared harder. "It's my job to make sure you're safe and not up to any daredevil stunts out there."

BB's warmth and concern shone through every word and made Morgan feel guilty at all the fun she'd had earlier.

"You're right. I'll be more careful in future," she promised. "I should've lit out when I saw him come up from behind his desk with the tire iron, but—"

"No buts." BB's leg pumped faster. "Sheesh! You scare five years off my life every time something like this happens."

Morgan leaned in next to Joe and whispered, "Which is why we don't tell her this stuff."

He nodded, but was more interested in watching BB's shoe dangle from the end of her foot. His eyes flared so hot Morgan felt the heat. BB's foot slowed to a stop while her gaze cut to his.

Morgan poured a cup of coffee. "Want some, BB?" She kept her voice husky, teasing her friend with the double entendre. Joe's neck reddened.

BB nodded, then uncrossed her legs and tucked them under the desk. Morgan slid BB's coffee under her nose. Her friend's face flamed under layers of foundation, bronzer and glittery blush. The mask had slipped. BB's makeup was no match for man-woman heat.

But Morgan didn't have the heart to tease her friend further—the undercurrents were too strong. BB was flummoxed by Joe Calder while Morgan was fascinated at their byplay.

She leaned over BB's shoulder to read the top sheet on the pile of work orders. BB, wise to the tactic, slammed her hand down so Morgan couldn't see it. Today's nail tips were purple with a line of gold at the edges.

"What have you got there?" Morgan asked, hoping for her next rush.

"I'll decide who goes where," BB said. "Back off." Her voice went low and tight. "I'm not kidding, Morgan. These are for the morning. You should go home. Both of you. You're done for today."

Not until she got a good look at that paperwork. After the fright on the last job, she was sure BB would hand her something too boring for spit.

"If you'd give us our work orders, we could head home," Joe said.

BB clicked her tongue, pulled the top sheet off the pile and held it out to Joe. "I'll give you this one." She flicked Morgan a defiant glance.

"Oh, for Pete's sake, just hand mine over," Morgan snapped, frustrated that all this hot need was not in her own life. Instead she fantasized about a man far removed from her day-to-day existence.

This was why she had to let Kingston McRae go the way of all teenage crushes. By keeping him uppermost in her mind, she put out *get lost* vibes around other men.

She read the sheet BB had handed her. "Not this guy again! How does he keep getting credit?" In spite of the economic slowdown, some people knew how to work the system.

BB shrugged. "Your guess is as good as mine. But at least he won't give you a hard time." They were up to three recoveries now and each time this man proved to be a happy-go-lucky sort. And b-o-r-i-n-g.

BB shifted in her seat as Joe headed through the opened counter, reading his work order. He snorted in derision. He obviously had a much more interesting job.

Morgan trailed him. "Where are you going?" She tried to peer around his chest to read his paperwork.

"Mercer Island."

"We don't get many recoveries there." The island held a lot of estates and mansions. "Is it a sports star or a news anchor?"

Joe scanned the sheet. "Kingston McRae."

Everything stilled, including Morgan's heart. His family home was here in Seattle, but he spent more time in

LA. Once her heart kicked back into gear, she stuttered, "Wh-who did you say?"

"I guess even tycoons can fall behind," Joe commented as he stepped outside. Before the door closed, she heard his last remark. "I doubt McRae will chase me with a tire iron, though."

Delicious adrenaline coursed through her and Morgan closed her eyes against the wash. He was at home.

And he was hers.

"Oh, no, you don't," BB said. "I know that expression, Morgan, and you cannot do what you're thinking."

"Watch me."

"I gave that work order to Joe because something weird will happen on that estate. Whatever it is, Joe can handle it." BB bit her lip.

This was her chance to get a real-life peek at Kingston McRae and Morgan would be damned if she let it slip out of her fingers. Her blood raced, her heart pounded and her impulsive love of the chase kicked into high gear.

She caught up to Joe just before he opened his truck door. She grabbed his arm and shoved the boring work order into his face. "We're trading."

"BB won't like it." His fingers held tight to his own order, but she tugged for all she was worth until he let go.

She held the paper to her chest. "BB's upset about the tire iron." She stepped out of his reach and smiled. "Nothing will go wrong on a Mercer Island estate." She glanced down at the sheet and shivered at the rush.

She'd be on Kingston McRae's home turf first thing in the morning. "I'll be in and out. Easy as pie. The man's on camera twenty-four seven. What could possibly go wrong?"

Joe narrowed his gaze. "Plenty. Dudes like McRae have security. Dogs, too. You could get messed up."

"Not a chance." She'd stay cool, calm. Keep her head on straight.

Even if she saw him.

She shivered again and headed for Bessie, her heart racing.

2

KINGSTON MCRAE STOOD at the window of his second-story home office and looked down on the front lawn and drive. The morning sun glinted off polished chrome, and he squinted for a better view of the car parked beneath the window. His fingers itched to hold that steering wheel. If it wasn't for this recent security problem, he'd take the shiny new Morgan for a test drive. He ran McRae Investments from home these days because he could. He did a lot of things because he could.

It was good to be him.

He wasn't used to denial, and he sure as hell didn't like it, but the test run had to wait.

He'd come home for Lindsay's wedding. Lindsay was his sister, not of blood, but very much of the heart. The Morgan was her surprise wedding gift, and if she didn't see him take it out for a run soon, she'd suspect something was up.

But right now he had to set Jack Carling on someone's trail. He tossed a set of photos onto his desk, faceup. "Mona of Twenty-four Carrot Catering found a package taped to her front door last night," he explained. "She brought these over at midnight, worried that I'd think she had something to do with them."

Jack used the tip of his pen to spread the photos out on the desk surface. He frowned as he read the words scrawled across them, one per photo: *You should have talked to me when I called.*

Nine photos in all, each scored by a pen. It had torn through the last one in a couple of spots.

"Whoever did this got angrier with every word," Jack observed.

"So it appears. The message could refer to those late-night calls before I left for Africa. I changed cell phone numbers and the calls stopped, but no one spoke." He snorted. "How could anyone expect me to speak when the line's silent?"

Jack examined the plain manila envelope the eight-by-tens had arrived in. "No markings except where the tape was used to stick it to Mona's front door. Her home or her office?"

"Home. She got in after a catering job at a radio station. Since there was no name on the envelope, she assumed it was for her. When she saw the photos of me arriving at the airport, she called and insisted on bringing them over right away."

Jack frowned more deeply. "I'll have these dusted for prints, see what else we can learn. Why deliver them to Mona?"

"I've worked with Mona on the QT for a year now. Using her is a clever way to get the message across."

Jack nodded. "That your private life isn't as private as you thought."

"You got it." That fact burned like acid, especially since he'd done everything possible to keep his philanthropy secret. He set Jack one more task. "Mona's upset that these photos arrived at her home. She has young children and is worried they might be at risk. I can't say I blame her. Set the family up somewhere else until we know more."

"Of course." Jack used a tissue to slide each photo back into the envelope. "I should have checked myself when you got those calls. I'll get Mona's fingerprints, so we can disregard hers on the envelope."

"As I recall, you put a new guy on it." Mac shrugged. "He came up empty." Jack had always been hard on himself. "They were run-of-the-mill calls, Jack. Nothing noteworthy."

"The calls were made from disposable phones. That should have been a red flag, especially for me." His face reddened.

"Don't sweat it. People get wrong numbers on cells all the time." Jack was his head of security but also one of his oldest friends so he felt personally responsible for Mac's safety. He put his hand on Jack's shoulder. "This isn't on you, Jack."

His friend shrugged him off. "How many calls did you get?"

"Three, maybe four, on consecutive nights. Three-fifteen as I recall, but it's been a couple months. I could be wrong. I was angry at the regularity. I lose enough sleep without being woken for nothing."

"They must have had access to the phone itself or they've got an in with your service provider. After seeing these photos, I'm convinced there's a connection—those calls weren't just wrong numbers. I'd also like to know how they found out you've been working with Mona."

"Not that hard, I suppose." Now that Mona's family would be taken care of, he felt more relaxed. "When I changed the number on the cell, the calls stopped." He slipped his hands into his pockets. "What's the threat, Jack? I don't see one." A few photos dropped off at the home of a woman he knew from his private mentoring program. Even with the vague references to phone calls, it didn't add up to much.

Jack gave a noncommittal grunt and tapped the envelope with his pen. "You have a stalker who has accelerated from calls to photos. You could be in danger."

Could be. "You, my friend, are losing it. You see danger where there is none. Idle hands and all that." Jack had been at loose ends ever since Mac had essentially retired from his high-pressure career. Mac had spent years rebuilding struggling companies. He'd done well and, having increased his net worth tenfold, was now ready to focus on what he loved best—mentoring neighborhood businesses with potential. Same type of work, but infinitely more satisfying.

Twenty-four Carrot Catering provided jobs where there were none before. Mona would soon be on her own, and Mac would find another start-up that needed help.

Jack looked ready to snarl, but Mac forestalled him. "There's no danger, Jack. A paparazzo did his homework and got a behind-the-scenes shot of me. Any moment now the phone will ring and I'll be asked to buy them."

"That makes sense if it weren't for the inherent threat in these words. And if your friend Mona hadn't been used to get the photos to you." Jack worked the snarl out of his voice. "You're not involved with her, are you?" His eyes narrowed. "She's married."

The question was ignored, as it deserved to be. Jack knew better than anyone that Mac's behavior was above reproach. He had strong reasons for living honorably and had never wavered. "If it's not a get-rich-quick paparazzo, it's just another fan with a crush, like the last two times." Mac shrugged, happy to have handed off the photos to Jack. He had a car to take out for a run. "Technology has made people too accessible."

"You're right, but if you'd give up this public image you've cultivated, you could have—"

"My parents tried flying under the radar, and it destroyed their marriage." His father had been a hypocrite: publicly happily married, but privately an unrepentant philanderer with questionable taste in women. When he was exposed, the marriage was destroyed, and along with it, any semblance of a normal childhood for Mac. He'd put the whole mess into perspective, but it still colored his attitude toward his family's high profile. Starting with a lumber baron great-grandfather who made his fortune through shady dealings and political connections, the McRae family had been in the public spotlight for generations.

His father's indiscretions and peccadilloes had brought out the worst kind of press. His mother's bitter disappointment at the public sniping destroyed her. She was a miserable wretch these days, who spent most of her time in an alcoholic haze.

At thirteen, Mac had been left to fend for himself until Rory, the loyal family majordomo, had stepped in as a father figure. Without Rory's dependable and loving influence, Mac could have gone all kinds of wrong. The deep connection between the men continued to this day.

"As long as I control what's reported about me," Mac said, "I keep my real life private." He focused on Hollywood exposure to make his home in Seattle a quiet retreat. Now that he worked mostly from home, he was grateful for the cover he'd built.

"In theory, it sounds fine," Jack agreed.

Until something happened to prove him wrong, he saw no reason to abandon a successful PR subterfuge. Not when the public believed all the fluff he fed them.

"In *theory* I should be allowed a private life, but I can't remember the last time I dated a woman just because I liked her."

Jack mimed playing a violin. "Yeah, the most beautiful women in Hollywood are at your beck and call and life's tough."

"At least it keeps the press from interfering with my mentoring program." Two years ago, Mac had taken his business skills to the streets. For special cases like Mona's catering business, he provided capital. His interests were varied, but small businesses provided jobs at the grassroots level. He loved what he did for free more than anything he'd ever done for money.

If enthusiastic but clueless entrepreneurs ever found out how much money he lent, he'd be inundated with requests, legitimate and otherwise. Only the most savvy owners saw that the real value was in Mac's advice, more than his money.

Jack grunted. Rubbed his face. "You're right, of course. If you didn't use the phoney playboy gambit as a screen, I'd be too busy with background checks on applicants to handle any real threats. Which reminds me, I want to replace the security system around the grounds. It's not up to snuff."

"We've got cameras everywhere. What's the problem?"

"They're five years old. The company that installed

them was sold last year. No way to know who's got access to their old files now."

Mac turned on his computer. State-of-the-art only months ago, it was already out of date. He should switch to the competition, but new software often made him wonder if he was running out of room in the cranium. "This should have been looked after before I got back." He sighed. "Look, all I want to do is take that dream car out for a test drive and make sure Lindsay's day is perfect tomorrow."

"I'll have a team of eight at the wedding. And I'll swap out the camera system."

"No team." Mac sat and clicked open his e-mail in-box. Jack had a habit of slipping information into the middle of a conversation. "Thought you'd get that by me, didn't you?"

Jack swore. "Someone's connected the dots of your life and come up with the right answers. You need security."

Mac considered. Whoever had taken the photos knew about his interest in local businesses and also when his jet had landed. They had also managed to be around his hangar, out of sight, to take the photos. This level of privacy invasion was a first, as was the vague threat.

Previous stalkers had been much more run-of-the-mill. Mac had received life-size nude photos of women. Panties, used and new, had arrived. Late-night knocks on hotel room doors had happened more often than he could count. These incidents had resulted from his public persona. For a stranger to see behind the facade to his private comings and goings was another matter.

No one had ever looked hard enough at his life to get this kind of information. Clearly, Jack was worried for Mac's personal safety this time.

"This person can get to you," Jack pressed. "We need to take the threat seriously. Also, whoever this is, they're smart."

Mac wasn't worried. "But not as smart as you. And there is no threat, just some scrawled words on photos. I don't read a threat there. You're overcompensating because you let a junior man handle those irritating phone calls and you blame yourself for this." He nodded at the package.

Jack stood. At five-ten he was shorter than Mac, but had twenty pounds on him. He smoothed his hair. "Mona's not the only one who should take off for a few days."

"Won't happen. I've got too much to catch up on." He couldn't ignore his domestic work any longer.

"How about Florida?"

"The house there is under renovation."

"With laborers all over the place, it won't be any more secure than here." Jack nodded. "And your villa in Spain is too accessible."

Mac loved the place, but it was beachfront—too public if someone wanted to get to him. "I'm anxious to dig in here with the locals again. Hands-on is what I enjoy most." He skimmed several e-mails that had been forwarded by his assistant in the main offices downtown. "As much as this will needle you, I want Lindsay's day to go as planned. No hulking security guys with earpieces."

Mac leaned back in his chair, feeling oddly sentimental and out of sorts because of it.

He wanted what Lindsay and Greg had. He wanted a connection with someone who saw the best in him, but knew the truth of him at the same time.

Jack still argued but Mac interrupted. "I will not allow

my security problem to ruin her day." Lindsay's parents had been killed in a car accident and her leg had suffered nearly irreparable damage. She'd also had to listen to her dying mother's cries until she was rescued. It had taken months for Lindsay to speak again. He banished the image of her, frail and blank-eyed in her hospital bed. She wasn't that child anymore.

"If Lindsay knew, you'd have to accept security."

He would not let a few photos and a vague threat cast a shadow on her day. "That's why you won't tell her about the stalker. Not a word, Jack."

His friend left, hackles raised and back stiff. Mac couldn't remember Jack this pissed before.

He thumbed through a stack of reports to find something to grab his attention, but remained unfocused. Unsettled. Unhappy.

Constricted by this stalker situation, he needed to blow off some steam. He could call an old flame. Forget it. The amount of effort it would take to get back into a woman's good graces made him scrub his face in frustration. Then he heard Jack's car fire up and peel off down the driveway.

The Morgan called to him. He'd take her out, see what she could do. Lindsay had found the spectacular British sports car on the Internet last year. Her face lit up at first sight of the classic lines and thirties styling. She'd moved on quickly to a car more in her price range, but Mac had taken note of her lust for the Morgan. Against his advice, she'd bought an affordable tin can. A decision he was pleased to correct.

But if he didn't take the car for a spin pretty soon, Lindsay might guess the Morgan was hers. As he stood up, he heard the click and rumble of a large diesel engine. Odd. He looked outside and watched a tow truck pull

in under the portico. The security monitor on his desk
showed the gates at the entrance to the property were
closed. How the hell…

Jack was gone and Rory was in his room for his final
tuxedo fitting. There was no one but Mac available to
see why the tow truck was here. He hadn't arranged for
it, and he'd know if there was a problem with one of the
vehicles.

The truck did a three-point turn, making it clear what
the driver was after. The Morgan! Mac glanced at the
front gate monitor again. This didn't make sense. If the
truck had come in as Jack was leaving he'd have seen it
and been on its ass all the way back up the drive.

The truck backed into position directly ahead of the
brand-new, specially ordered Morgan Plus 4.

Like hell they'd get that car! Mac took off at a dead
run, down the stairs, and careened to a halt by the front
door. He slid on the freshly polished marble, but saved
himself from a header by grabbing the handle. He yanked
the door open and strode outside in his socks.

"Hey, you!" Anger roiled in his gut at the sheer audacity of the thief. A sexy *female* thief in the tightest,
shortest pair of shorts he'd ever seen.

The woman was bent over between the tow truck and
the Morgan, ass in the air. He snapped his mouth shut
and took in the stunning view while his mind blanked
out.

Every boy's dream came to life before his eyes and
he couldn't quite take it in: a big truck and a pretty girl.
Together. He had a thing for Daisy Duke short shorts,
ever since watching reruns of good ol' boys and their
sexy cousin when he was ten.

But this was no rerun. This was here and now and
she was a flesh-and-blood woman, tilted so perfectly

he could see the fleshy mounds at the top of each leg. Flesh that bloomed into a pair of cheeks that sat high and round on the top of a great set of shapely feminine legs. If he wasn't so antsy to find out what she thought she was doing, he'd stay there a moment just to enjoy a glimpse of fine female butt.

He must be suffering brain freeze, because he *had* been standing there enjoying the sight of her!

Which was exactly what she wanted.

She moved each knee slowly, one after the other, making her ass cheeks move and sway. Another couple seconds of observation couldn't hurt.

She swayed her ass again, this time with her legs slightly apart. Heat spiked in his groin.

The ploy was obvious, so he dug deep for control. "Hey, there, need a hand?" he asked, cool and quiet to keep his temper in check and his libido under control. He hadn't increased the family fortune by letting sex or anger color his actions.

Her head came up a fraction at his question. A mop of auburn hair cascaded to her shoulders. He'd always been partial to red.

"Thanks for the offer." Her voice came sultry soft and poker hot. "But I'll just keep at it."

He responded the way any normal red-blooded male would. His blood rushed south of his waist and his mouth went dry, while his brain kicked into caveman mode. That dark, primal side of him wanted to drag her into his lair and keep her there until he was done with her, but the civilized half of his brain demanded patience.

His palms broke into a sweat. Three months was a long time to be away. Even longer in Africa, where a man didn't take chances with sex. No wonder his caveman wanted to take charge.

He stepped closer, caught her fresh soap scent on the breeze, and his libido strained for the finish line. He cleared his throat. "What do you think you're doing? Because you're sure as hell not getting away with my car."

"I'm doing my job." She tossed the words over her shoulder with a quick jab to his ego. The tone said she'd used the line too many times to count. He caught a flash of dark eyes, but she straightened immediately, as if she'd felt a boot to her rear end.

She kept her back to him and sidestepped to the side of the tow truck. Her gloved hand landed on one of several control sticks with large round knobs on top. The movement emphasized her trim waist and womanly round hips. She shifted the controller and a bar slowly dropped to the ground behind the truck. She bent over farther to place the bar between the Morgan's front wheels, snapping his attention back to her butt.

He couldn't remember a time when he'd felt so ignored.

She looped straps around the left front tire and used S hooks to secure the straps to the T-bar. No chains, no giant hook. He hadn't looked at a tow truck in years. Not since childhood, when all trucks had fascinated him the way they would any boy.

If it wasn't *his* car being stolen, he might want to see how this all worked.

He should call the police, or at the very least Jack, but he'd left his cell phone on his desk. If he so much as blinked, this woman would hightail it down the drive with Lindsay's Morgan.

"How did you get in here?" he asked. He kept his tone conversational. "The gates are closed." He'd checked the monitor himself.

"You sure about that?"

Her smooth competent manner made him doubt what he'd seen. He stepped out onto the drive to take a look. At the end of the quarter-mile lane, the double gates stood open. "But the monitor— Hell! You stay right where you are." His security had been hacked. Jack would love being right.

He stepped back to the front door, reached inside and pressed the button to close the gates. With satisfaction he locked the woman, her truck and the Morgan inside the estate with him.

"You're not taking my Morgan. Tell me how you hacked my security cameras." He pointed to the gates as they swung shut.

A satisfying fear flashed into her eyes. Now he had her attention. No more being ignored.

But instead of fluttering her hands or backing up, she took the five steps required to bring her within kissing range and poked him in the chest. Hard.

"Hey. No need to get physical." Under the courageous glint in her eyes, a conflicting storm of emotion brewed. She was torn between interest in him and determination to do her job, whatever it was. He recognized that determination. As for the interest, it mirrored his own. He hid a smile.

Maybe it wasn't interest he saw. Maybe she was starstruck. He'd seen it before.

Up close her eyes weren't as dark as he'd first thought. They were a shade of green that often came with auburn hair—common if it weren't for the flare of sherry around the iris. Her chin fanned into a square jaw that some women wore well. On a man it would be strong; on a woman it was sexy as Mother Nature could make it.

This woman was tightly packed, beautifully formed

and perfectly toned. She wore her thick hair parted in the middle, framing an arresting face free of makeup.

Poke. She jabbed him again, while flinty eyes glared up into his. "No need to get physical? You let me out of here, or I'll show you physical!"

So, not starstruck. Angry. Maybe even frightened at being caught red-handed.

"Do not poke me again." He gave her his most intimidating glare. "That's assault. You could be arrested. Correct that. You *will* be arrested."

"You wouldn't dare."

He caught her raised finger before she could use it. Her hand was small, like the rest of her, but strong. She freed herself from his grasp.

Good thing, because he'd damn near pulled her closer.

3

TWICE! SHE'D POKED Kingston McRae *twice!* Her hand flamed where he'd touched her, and for a split second she thought she saw desire flash behind his eyes.

Up close, he was more manly, more intimidating, more dangerous than she'd imagined. Frustration boiled under his skin, the heat of it releasing his scent.

More than hazel, his eyes were shot through with gold. Bristly and unshaven, his chin looked rough and her skin reacted viscerally as she conjured it scraping and sliding over her delicate flesh. Oh, mama! His sexual power called out to her female instincts in ways she'd only dreamed about.

Kingston McRae had never been more than an abstract, an unreachable, untouchable impossibility. And here she was: reaching, touching, *poking* him. The man. The very real, very potent man.

His attempt to intimidate her nearly worked. But she grounded herself with a reminder that she was here to do her job. "I shouldn't have poked you," she said. "I apologize. I, uh, react before I think sometimes."

Was it any wonder? Kingston McRae in the flesh!

Her brain felt like a frozen slush drink, thick and barely moving.

Get a grip, woman, he's only a man. A man like any other who defaulted on a payment. He responded to the situation the same way they all did. That meant she could respond by rote. Her slow brain didn't have to work. She kicked it into automatic.

"I have every right to take the car," she explained. "The papers are on the clipboard." Out of her depth, and starstruck, she did what she always did. Got tough. "Read 'em yourself. Everything's in order."

She tilted her head in the direction of the truck cab.

"If you'd just look at the papers instead of staring at me, you'd see for yourself."

He blinked. Different colored pages fluttered in the morning breeze. Eyes dark as thunder, Kingston McRae catalogued her from her head to her toes and a frisson of awareness followed.

The fact that he'd closed her only way out plucked a nerve. "Open the gates."

He glanced at the clipboard and she noticed a muscle jump in his jaw while he considered her request. "I need some answers first."

She should call BB. But her friend would blow a gasket if she learned Morgan had broken her number one rule: Never go anywhere without telling the office first.

And also the second rule: Never trade paperwork without telling BB.

The longer she could avoid that whole mess, the better.

"If you don't want to read the paperwork yourself, get someone else to do it. You do have other people to take care of this stuff, don't you?" And there was the difference between this pickup and every other one she'd done. He probably didn't even handle his own money.

He opened his mouth, but closed it again without a word.

"Before you ask, yes, I know who you are." Then she turned on her heel and walked to the far side of her rig.

"Bessie," he said, reading the name she'd had lettered in rolling script on the side of the truck bed. "That's short for Elizabeth. My mother's name."

Taken aback by the change in tone from brusque to easygoing, she responded, "My mother's, too." But her mother hated the shortened form, considered it low class. But it had grown on Morgan, and now she rarely saw the connection between the two names. Bessie was her rolling, rollicking baby while Elizabeth lived with husband number seven in a Florida condo, far away from Seattle.

"So it's not your name?" he asked.

Out of the corner of her eye she saw him pick up the clipboard and read the top page of the work order.

"No, it's not my name." She took in his strong profile as he read. From the side, she saw his lips firm, and again that telltale muscle jumped in his jaw.

"I paid for this car myself!" he blurted. Shock colored his tone belligerent, which suited her just fine. Belligerent was familiar. Belligerent she could handle.

"I'm sure it's just a mix-up, then." Her tone was practiced and bland. "But, still, it's my responsibility to pick up the car. You can sort out the mess after I leave." She bent to loop the straps around the right tire.

"It's rude not to face a person when they speak to you," he said as he watched her drop to her haunches to connect the S hooks.

"Like I said, it's a mix-up." She smoothed her moist palms on her backside as she rose to face him across Bessie's back end.

Her face felt warm. She must look glowing and eager, but she refused to palm her cheeks and look even more foolish. With luck she'd get through this without drooling. She peered over his left shoulder, a trick she used to keep her impulsive nature in check, but it was impossible to treat him like an anonymous defaulter. He was Kingston freaking McRae, her very own version of Prince Charming in the flesh. Her heart raced and a new kind of adrenaline pulsed through her veins.

Determined not to fall over from his blast of handsome, she shifted her gaze to his and prayed that he'd wave her away. "Open the gates, Mr. McRae. There's no way you can fight this." Many had tried, all had failed. "If it's a mistake, and I'm sure it is, you'll sort it out with the bank. The car will be back here in no time. You'll see." There, she'd given him his out. Most people used the bank error excuse to save face.

Mac scanned the woman's features. She was serious. Her deadpan delivery proved it. She'd said these same things many times. To her, he was just another in a long line of people having vehicles repossessed. She didn't care who he was. A job was a job was a job to her.

She didn't know he was in the midst of a security crisis and she might be an unwitting pawn. Jack was right, the photos were just the beginning. This was a personal attack. First the pictures were delivered to Mona, then his security on the gates was compromised, and now his payment for the Morgan was somehow invalid. This paperwork looked legitimate. And this woman believed she was here to do her job, when what she was unwittingly doing was delivering another message.

Jack needed to know about this right away.

But until Mac knew how his payment had been rigged, he couldn't let her leave.

Especially not with the Morgan.

Her lively, intelligent gaze filled with heated interest that ricocheted down to his groin. The tilt to her chin and her straight back indicated an inner struggle to stay focused on the job.

Her expression was made up of three parts confidence and one part defiance. Most women he knew were polished enough to be coy and flirtatious. But this one? Didn't have a coy bone in her body. "I'll get Rory, my personal assistant, out here to confirm payment. He'll get the bank on the phone."

Mac ran his fingers through his hair, determined to prove payment was made. He'd transferred the funds himself before he left for Africa. A quick call was all that was needed to save the day, but until then, he'd be happy to keep his eye firmly on the woman.

"The car will be back before you know it." She gave him a cool smile and climbed into the truck cab. Sitting sideways so that her legs dangled outside, she stretched for the radio on the dash. She held a thumb over the talk button. "Now, open the gates or I'll have the police here."

"You're serious." He stepped to back toward the house, holding up a hand to delay her. Tempted to call her bluff, he considered the uproar in the tabloids if his estate was swarmed by officers. "You must see that this is not your usual situation with deadbeats."

She nodded. "Most people don't want me to stick around. They want me and my truck off the property."

Her matter-of-fact behavior convinced him she wasn't part of some scheme to steal his car. This was more likely a hack by his stalker. Damn, Jack would tear a strip off him for having been cavalier about this. After his friend laughed long and hard.

He pressed the intercom that connected him to Rory's rooms and asked him to bring a phone to the front door. "Thanks, Rory. We have a situation that needs your immediate attention."

He wanted to know her name. Probably a reaction to the way she'd ignored him, but there it was. He got what he wanted. Always. He'd learned how to circumvent obstacles at sixteen when he'd taken on the medical establishment to help get Lindsay back on her feet. That lesson in dogged determination had served him well in business, and it would serve him well with this auburn-haired beauty.

God, she was sexy. She wore a light gray T-shirt with a row of open buttons down the front that showed enough cleavage to make him think of the Grand Canyon.

He moved close to the truck door. A vanilla scent wafted by his nose. He strained for more, but it was gone after one whiff.

Her smooth tanned knees were now at his chest height and he struggled to keep from staring at them. Tried to stop imagining them open in invitation.

She blew out a breath. "This personal assistant of yours had better hurry because the day's half gone and you're not the only pickup I have."

"But I bet it's the only one you've got in *this* neighborhood. You can wait five minutes." She was raw and rough and sassy as hell and he enjoyed every bit of it. It was all he could do to suppress a grin.

His comment brought a tilt to one corner of her mouth

but she refused to respond with more. Instead, she removed her short beige leather work gloves. Strong, capable hands that had felt fragile and small in his. Plain, unadorned hands. No polish. No rings. How had he missed that salient fact earlier?

He handed her the clipboard. She took it from him, careful not to brush his fingers, then set it on the littered dashboard.

"Now, tell me how you got in here."

"Easy. As soon as the suit left I scooted up the driveway."

"Scooted in this thing?" He patted the heavy door.

"Okay, so scooted isn't exactly the right word—more like booted it up the driveway."

"But *the suit* would have seen you make a dash. He'd have followed you back in."

She shook her head. "He didn't." She checked her nonexistent manicure. "And the gate was open all morning, ever since the suit arrived." She shifted to face front, but kept her left leg outside in an enticing dangle.

"How long did you wait?"

She swung her leg back and forth in a tick-tock motion. His gut tightened with each seductive swing of her booted foot.

Tick tock.

Tick.

Tock.

Abstinence had gotten to him if her feminine version of ankle-high work boots seemed erotic. Tan leather laced to the top, heavy socks rolled down to a neat fold, they made him hot. He rubbed the back of his neck to try to reverse the flow of blood from his head. "Why didn't you follow Jack in when he arrived?"

"I wanted to wait for your guest to leave before I

picked up the car." She blinked and went pink in the cheeks. Amazing. "I didn't want to cause you embarrassment by showing up in the middle of something important. I appreciate this is a private matter for you."

Special treatment never surprised him, but her sensitivity did. Until now she'd been blunt and matter-of-fact. He shied away from calling it *rude* because there were times he was just as direct.

She swung her leg as if it helped contain some of the nervous energy that crackled around her. *Tick. Tock.*

"Where did you hide?" he asked to keep his mind off her leg.

"Across the street beside that big bush that needs a trim." She frowned. "You've done a good job distracting me, but your time's up. You can't keep me locked in here," she said as she pressed down the talk button on the handset. The radio crackled to life.

He reached in, covered her hand with his and looked deep into her green eyes. Her breath caught and that vanilla scent blew over him. Unfortunately, he hadn't made adjustments for her swinging leg. It caught him between the legs. "Oof!"

"Sorry," she murmured, and bent her knee to give him room.

"No harm done," he muttered. The handset fell into his palm as he shifted his hips out of harm's way. Good God, the woman was exquisite up close. Her cheeks went the same shade of pink he'd seen before while the rest of her face paled to white. Her lips were moist and perfect and far too close, but he couldn't move away as he fought the urge to lean in closer and take...

"Tell me your name." She reached for the handset as his fingers closed around it. Her lips parted and he wanted to dive in to take her mouth with his. Then he wanted to crawl on top of her and press her into the seat. Wanted to feel her wrap those incredible legs around him. Wanted those sexy booted feet in the air.

But Rory was on his way, and until he knew exactly how his system had been breached, he needed to focus.

He had to be as focused as she was.

He picked up the sound of Rory's footsteps and asked again, softly, "Your name?"

"Morgan. Morgan Swann." She rolled her eyes and feigned innocence.

"This is a joke."

She shook her head. "Nope. Ironic, right?"

He looked at the car, then back at her. "Ironic, yes." He heard a throat clear behind him. Rory. Time had run out.

"What's going on?" Rory asked.

Mac wasn't sure if he meant the tow truck or the way he'd all but climbed into the cab with a gorgeous woman. Heat glowed in the depths of her green gaze and he had no desire to leave.

"Sir?" Rory asked again. "What's happening with the Morgan?"

"I wish I knew," he muttered. Her eyes went from hot to good-humored just before he turned to Rory. "Morgan here—" he stepped aside so Rory could see her "—claims the Morgan there—" he gestured toward the car "—hasn't been paid for. She's here to repossess it." He couldn't mention the stalker in front of Morgan. That was private business and Jack would see to it.

"The term is *recover,*" she clarified. "I recover property." She stared, awestruck, at Rory, who looked resplendent in his tuxedo. The old man cleaned up well. "And you're wearing a tuxedo. In the morning!"

It was the utter shock in her tone that finally wrecked Mac's control. He laughed, long and hard, and dodged another poke in the chest.

He grabbed her hand before she could pull it back. "Not this time," he said, and kissed her fingertip.

"Hey," she protested and drew her hand back. She looked at her finger. "Point taken. No more poking."

The older man sputtered, "Poking? She's poking you?" Then he stared down at his tuxedo. "This is for—" His eyes went wide. "Never mind why I'm dressed like this." He assessed Morgan with a hard-ass expression.

"BB WARNED ME ABOUT this job going weird," Morgan muttered. She'd swear nothing this strange had ever happened to a Five Aces driver before.

The rich *were* different. It was easy to see why the fancy-dressed man oozed competence and command. He leveled a gaze meant to intimidate her. "Mr. McRae arranged for the funds himself."

"Which confirms exactly nothing. I still have to take it."

The butler bristled but Morgan refused to budge. If she left without the car she would have to admit to BB that she'd switched jobs with Joe, and come here without anyone knowing. Then Joe would be in as much trouble as Morgan and that wasn't fair or right. She had to stick to her guns and get this car out of here.

"The video feed to my security monitor has been tampered with, Rory."

Rory blanched. "But how?"

"That's one of several questions for the day."

"But I just checked the monitors. Everything looks fine."

"It's supposed to. Please call Jack. He'll look into it. You've got more important things to deal with today."

Rory gave him a tight smile. "That I do." He made the call on the portable phone he'd brought out with him. He repeated the news about the monitor video feeds and wound everything up with her arrival to *recover* the Morgan. "Yes, sir, thank you," he said into the phone.

There was more going on here than she knew, but since it wasn't any of her business, she pretended not to hear a thing.

When Rory hung up, his gaze cut to Kingston. "Mr. Carling will return right away, sir."

"Thank you, Rory." His tone surprised her. He was calm and polite with Rory. Patient, too. This low rumbling purr was his real voice, the one he used with those he cared about. She hadn't heard it until now.

"It's possible there's more happening here than a missed payment or simple bank error, Ms. Swann," Kingston said.

No kidding! "Look—" She held up both hands. "I'm sorry for your troubles but I need my job. And right now, my job hinges on me sliding myself and my truck right on out of here with the Morgan along for the ride." Any moment one of them would step back to the door and push whatever button operated the gates. If they thought her job really was on the line, they'd let her go. When neither of them moved, she pressed the issue again. "You have no right to hold me here." Avoiding BB's long-term wrath was worth the white lie about her job.

Kingston moved in close again. She closed her eyes to lessen his effect on her breathing. No good. His voice went low and soft, trickling seduction along her nerve endings. "This is an attack on my security system and on my personal accounts at the least. It could get worse before it gets better. Can't you see your way clear to wait until we sort out the car?"

She peeped one eye open and found him staring at her. The man was too much! Demanding and autocratic one minute, reasonable and kind another. Now she saw a man who needed her understanding. She sank toward compliance, unable to deny him when he needed help. "Will you do that, Morgan? Will you wait while we sort this out?"

She swallowed hard at the sound of her name spoken with that rumbling tone and nodded. "Getting the Morgan to the impound yard this morning seems less likely by the minute, but I'll keep it rigged to Bessie if you don't mind." If she called Joe and asked him to avoid the office for the time being, she'd buy time.

"Rory, could you please explain to Miss Swann—" Kingston stared at her. "It is Miss, isn't it?" His gaze cut to her naked ring finger.

Her heart stalled as she squeaked out a reply. "Yes, I'm single. Completely single." Nothing like advertising. Damn her mouth.

The heat in his gaze stole another breath as her heart kicked in again. If this kept up, she'd be dizzy in no time.

The older man gave her a stern look. He seemed as outraged as most men when she did her job. "I'll call the bank immediately."

"Thank you," Kingston said with a smile as Rory turned to leave. "Let us know what you learn."

Rory strode into the house, his shoulders squared, back straight, although he must be seventy-plus.

"Some men would automatically suspect the help," she said. At least, that's the impression she had of the extremely wealthy. The *World Courier* was full of stories of obnoxious behavior from movie stars and supermodels.

He chuckled and shook his head. "Rory? Cheat me? Not a chance."

His eyes warmed to caramel when he was amused. She could never learn *that* from a tabloid.

"My friends call me Mac."

"Oh." Her belly dropped because he felt the easy comfort between them, too. A moment of connection. A blink in time but a lifetime to her.

"Could someone have stolen your identity? Caused mischief that way?" she suggested in spite of her decision to stay out of his problems.

"You mean with the car payment. It's possible, I suppose. I thought this was a security breach at first, but you may be right." He frowned. "It's been an odd morning to say the least."

She shrugged. "Identity theft happens a lot these days. Or you sometimes hear stories about people who pretend to be relatives of—" She shut up. He didn't want to hear her thoughts.

"Celebrities? The wealthy?" He raised his eyebrows.

"They pretend to be sons, cousins, even heirs to fortunes."

"I don't have any brothers." He gave a lopsided grin. "That I know of, anyway."

"It's another way to look at the problem. We don't make mistakes at Five Aces, um, Mac." Her cheeks warmed when she used the familiar form of his name. "If we have this paperwork, you can bet that somewhere there's an account that shows you didn't pay your bill."

"Beautiful and smart. Thanks for the suggestion. I'll get Jack on it right away...*Morgan.*"

Her cheeks burned hotter. "Jack's the suit?" she guessed.

"Jack Carling, the head of my security team."

"Ha! You better rethink that position. 'Cause he's doing the dog on this one."

He cocked one eyebrow and took the moment from warm and friendly to hot and intense in a heartbeat. "He'll be hard enough on himself about all of this. He doesn't need any reminders from me."

Surprised at his attitude toward what anyone else might consider a major inconvenience, she made a show of checking her watch. "Will Mr. Carling be here soon? I can give you a few minutes, but no longer."

He nodded and his face lit up with a breathtaking smile. She'd seen his smile in photos, but aimed at her in the bright light of day, it had nuclear force.

She should have been long gone by now, but she'd wasted precious seconds when she'd caught a glimpse of him at the upstairs window. She'd gone into a fantasy-induced stupor at the idea of meeting him. She could have had the Morgan under way in thirty seconds, but instead, she'd stalled out like a gushing schoolgirl.

Who was she kidding? She'd left her hair down, shaved her legs and moisturized with her favorite vanilla-scented body lotion this morning just on the off chance she'd get a peek at the man. In her wilder moments of wildest fantasy she hadn't come up with this scenario.

She never imagined Kingston McRae looking at her as if she were an ice cream treat on a hot day.

He slid his hands into his trouser pockets, eyes caught on hers in male interest. If they hadn't locked horns over his car, they might be locking lips.

"Then again," she said with a grin, "this may not be the suit's fault. Maybe I'm good at my job."

He grinned at that. "I'm sure you are. And I think that as far as you and Five Aces are concerned, the paperwork's legitimate."

"Sometimes an unlucky ex gets snagged up in a web of legal nonsense and underhanded credit scams out of vengeance. Do you have a woman who's mad at you?"

"I make no promises to women." His lip quirked. "Besides, I don't believe you'd go along with something this underhanded."

"I'd be straight up if I was piss—ticked off with a man. If I'd been left—"

"So, this isn't personal between you and me."

"Of course not!" What she wouldn't give to get personal, though.

"The good thing is, I've never set eyes on you before—"

She blustered an interruption. "Of course you haven't. We don't exactly run in the same circles, you and I."

"—because if I'd ever seen you before I'd remember you."

"Oh." She didn't know what to make of that, so she looked at her feet.

Then his.

He was in his socks. Very *nice* socks. Expensive.

She felt his searing stare and melted into a puddle of hormones. Kingston McRae was mind-bogglingly handsome in real life. Vibrant and bright, he was hard planes and smooth strength in a package topped by burnished oak hair with matching eyes.

Eyes that widened with pure let-me-at-it male interest when she let her glance travel up from his socks to his face. He was bigger and more solidly built in person than he looked in the tabloids. Those pictures never did him justice. And the tuxedos he wore to movie premieres hid most of his muscles. Morgan got an eyeful now. Oh, Mama!

Every dream she'd let shatter and scatter over the past seven years now re-formed as sharp and clear as they'd ever been.

Oh, get a grip! What she felt was not about dreams or being swept off her feet. It was lust, pure and simple. Her sex twitched, her breath rattled, her face heated.

From the focused male expression on Kingston McRae's face, he was on the other end of this arc of desire.

Like the pot of gold at the end of a rainbow, he waited.

Wanted.

Just like her.

4

"THIS *RECOVERY* COULD be an embarrassment, if the tabloids pick up on it." Kingston's statement held a question.

"I understand," Morgan said. She'd never share her impressions of him with the public. Well, maybe BB. But she could trust her friend to keep quiet. "The *World Courier* would punish you for months with this. From what I've seen in tabloids lately, *punish* is the right word."

"You've seen that rag?"

"Only the headlines while I'm at the cash desk." She refused to admit she pored over the articles and pictures.

"It's one thing to speculate on my deliberately public romances, but it's dirty to go after my personal financial situation."

She leaned against Bessie, trying to ignore the broad hint about deliberately public romances. Did he mean the stories about him being a playboy were phony? Was he nothing like his reputation? *Stick to the point, Swann!* "If it helps, in spite of my past experience with deadbeats, I believe you believe the car's paid for."

"You just called me a deadbeat." He looked thunder-struck, then immediately chuckled. "You're priceless."

"Most people find the term—" she shrugged "—insult-ing. Sorry, I shouldn't have said it." She couldn't believe she *had* said it. But she was flustered, turned on, and her deeply buried feminine side rose to the surface.

The side of her that had made her forego her ball cap this morning. The side that encouraged her to wash, mousse and curl her hair. The side that made her put on her only set of matching bra and panties. Feeling pretty under her clothes boosted her confidence.

No point tamping that sexual side back down either. Once that siren was released, there was no stopping her.

In spite of her inner vixen and no matter what had happened while he was away in "parts unknown," as reported in the tabloid, it was still her job to impound the car. After that, the lender and the debtor had to sort things out.

"I won't speak of this," she offered earnestly. "Not anywhere, not to anyone. You have my word. This is between you, your bank and the dealership you bought from."

He ran his fingers through his hair and mussed it into peaks she wanted to smooth.

Her fingers itched to touch his lightly bristled chin and his mussed hair, so she grabbed her gloves off the dashboard and pulled them back on. For the life of her, she couldn't remember taking them off.

He looked down the drive again and she tracked his gaze. A black Crossfire pulled up to the closed gates. A man's arm reached out, punched in a code and the gates swung open. "They're working now," she said. But just as she'd seen this morning, after the car roared through, the gates stayed open.

"See?" she said.

"I see." He stepped back to the door and used an intercom to call Rory. "Check the monitors one more time, will you, Rory?" He waited a moment, then swore.

The Crossfire slowed to a stop and Mr. Carling, who must feel the fool, climbed out. "Nice car," she said to Mac. "Shame they stopped building them."

He raised an eyebrow. "A car buff?"

"Something like that."

The security chief had parked in front of Bessie and was now on his phone. She shook her head in derision. "If I have to, I'll drive over the lawn to get around him."

"I bet you would."

"I said I'd stay and answer his questions, so it's cool." She faced the Morgan. "She's beautiful. If I had her I'd give her a name."

"Not Bessie," Mac said, with a twitch at the corner of his mouth.

"Not Bessie. Something sleek and sexy to go with her glamorous lines. A classic, classy name would suit her." If she asked nicely and explained the situation, BB might look at the paperwork again and offer to help from her end. She could yell at Morgan all she wanted afterward.

"Althea maybe? Or Diana?"

"Hortense," she said.

Mac laughed and rocked back on his heels. "How about Bella?"

"That's better than Hortense."

"Stay where you are," the security chief commanded from behind her. She turned in surprise as he slipped his cell phone into his pocket. He'd obviously been running her plate and checking out Five Aces. A worm of fear wriggled in her belly at the idea. She never liked it when people looked past what she wanted them to see. "We've got questions," he said.

"No shit, Sherlock." She bristled just looking at this guy. "I have the right to leave, I have the right to take this car. There's the paperwork." She pointed to the clipboard on the seat. "Mac's already seen it."

"Mac?" The use of the more familiar name shocked him enough to stop him cold. He glared at Mac, then dropped his brows into a dark frown. "What the hell?"

Mac was all business now, stern and uncompromising. He'd only wanted to keep her entertained until this Jack guy got back. All the steamy looks had just been a cover to forestall her taking the Morgan.

Her ego deflated like a month-old balloon as he went to the door to close the gates. In the distance, she saw them move. "Morgan's offered to answer our questions, Jack, so back off."

Jack Carling watched the gates operate from the manual switch. "They should have closed after I passed through. So that answers how she got in to take your car. And it also shows that the security problem isn't just with the monitor or camera system." He swore. "Mac, you're the target of a systematic attack."

"Could be," he said. Jack turned to glare at her.

Morgan didn't care for the way this guy sized her up and found her wanting. He even sneered at Bessie.

"How long have you been stalking Kingston McRae?" he demanded.

She heated with guilt. She had a crush, a silly girly crush, but stalking? "You're out of your mind," she snapped.

"SHE'S NOT MY STALKER, Jack," Mac defended her as she deserved to be defended. He swiveled his attention from the delectably shocked Morgan to his security chief. "And this is not the way to get our questions answered." Jack must be spooked if he'd lost his cool detachment.

Morgan's eyes flashed indignation. "Mac's right. I may not be some la-di-da red-carpet beauty, but I know my job. And I'm good at it." Her voice went low and firm and her eyes shot sparks. "This car's not paid for." She swept her arm in an arc to showcase the Morgan, dangling from the rear of her truck. "So it's coming with me."

She set her chin and narrowed her eyes. And looked to Mac like more woman than any *la-di-da red-carpet beauty* he'd ever seen. Her unpainted face glowed with confidence and inner strength. There was no speck of artifice in this Morgan Swann. She was the epitome of *what you see is what you get* and he stood back and enjoyed the sheer gutsy determination of the woman.

But no matter how strong or determined she looked, the Morgan would not leave his property, not when it was needed for the wedding tomorrow. The woman had been prepared to be reasonable until Jack arrived.

Faced with Morgan's determined expression and aggressive stance, Jack actually stepped back. Her five foot three suddenly looked a lot taller. Mac controlled a laugh because he knew exactly how the dynamo on full attack could affect a man.

He frowned. Jack might react to Morgan the same way Mac had.

And he didn't like the idea. Not a bit.

"Jack, meet Morgan Swann. Morgan's got some great suggestions on where to start our investigation." She'd come up with identity theft and a phoney relative scam to start. He hadn't even mentioned the stalker and she'd offered up ideas.

He wanted to freeze-frame Jack's shock so he could rib him about it later.

The expression of warmth and appreciation on Morgan's face made his mouth water. He wanted his hands on her. He wanted his lips on her. He wanted hers on him.

Her light green eyes rounded. "Mac? You heard my ideas?" She sounded out of breath, as if the stand-off with Jack had cost her. It probably had.

He smiled at her, caught by the unguarded expression in her gaze. Warm, interested. Genuine. Uncomplicated.

"Of course I thought they were viable."

"What the hell's going on here?" Jack demanded.

"Lots." He explained about the video feeds, gave him a brief update on Morgan's suggestions about identity theft and even her theory on an impostor posing as a relative. Jack looked nonplussed at the various ideas.

Then he moved toward the front door. "Miss Swann, if you wouldn't mind coming inside," he said, his tone conciliatory, his eyes flint sharp. "You may be able to help me, uh, help Mac with these problems." He motioned for her to enter the house.

She turned, reached into the front seat and pulled out a denim satchel, then allowed the men to usher her inside. When Jack moved a hand to her back, she froze until he released her. She stepped through the doorway alone and proud.

Jack glared at him as if Mac had lost his mind.

"Wow, this is beautiful, all right," Morgan said, cataloguing the grand foyer. "Do you mind if I freshen up?"

Her earnest comment made him look at the place with

a jaundiced eye. "Beauty isn't always what it seems." Cool and sterile, the house still had his mother's stamp on it. He'd been too busy to warm it up. "There's a guest washroom behind the stairs." He directed Morgan to it.

He'd never much cared for this place, but Rory was used to it and with Lindsay living here until her marriage, he'd held on to the home. But after the wedding, he'd look into selling.

He and Rory could share a large single-level. They'd move before stairs became a nuisance for the older man.

"You've lost it, my friend," Jack said as soon as they were alone, "if you assume this woman is no threat."

"Read the paperwork. It looks official. Rory's on the phone with the bank now. Our computer system's been compromised. The monitors show the gates closed when they aren't. Whoever this is, they mean business." He frowned. "Morgan Swann's too bright to expose herself this way if she wanted to do me harm." From what he'd just seen of her, if she was ticked with him, she'd be upfront about it.

Jack sighed. "Yeah, she's more likely to punch you in the nose straight on than be devious."

"You saw that, too, huh?"

"She's one tough cookie. Besides, you have no connection to her. She's got no reason to go after you this way. This is personal." Jack dug in his pocket for his phone and started a call to his IT expert. "And you, my friend, should stop looking at her like she's a hot fudge sundae. You can't encourage a strange woman. Phone calls and pictures are one thing, but now we know you've been targeted. Until we know who and why, you've got to lay low."

He'd planned to spend the morning at his corporate head office, but an image of Morgan's short shorts, hot leather gloves and tanned muscular legs popped into his head. "I'll stay home today. I can find something to do."

"Or some*one* to do." Jack leaned in to give him a low-voiced piece of advice. "Just not her, Mac. Just not her."

MORGAN TOOK HER TIME washing her hands in the guest washroom. She needed a few moments to regroup. The second Mac had done the unimaginable and leaned all over her in Bessie's cab, she'd gone mushy inside. That would not do.

When she'd switched paperwork with Joe, she'd wanted to get a look at Mac's house, maybe catch a distant glimpse of him.

But being accused of stalking him was off-the-charts crazy. No way could buying a few tabloids be construed as stalking. If that were true, then half of America was stalking some celebrity or other.

But Mac had defended her on nothing more than a first impression. Warmed by the intensity of his gaze, she splashed cold water on her wrists to cool her raging pulse.

After drying her hands, she called Joe. "Hi, it's Morgan. I hope you haven't been to the office yet."

"I'm here now."

She groaned. "Don't tell BB where I am, okay?"

"She figured it out when I turned in the car you should have picked up this morning." He kept his voice low. "I've never seen that shade of furious before. She's trying to call your cell right now, cursing you out because it's busy."

She squeezed her eyes shut to help her think. There was no way she'd leave now, not for BB, not for Joe. Being in Mac's home brought her fantasies infinitely closer to coming true.

No man looked at a woman the way he'd looked at her without wanting sex. If she denied what she'd seen in his eyes, then she should hand in her union card to the department of femininity. No way would she leave without seeing where this visit could lead. "Sorry I got you into trouble with BB, but I can't leave yet. There's some stuff…" Stuff she couldn't explain, and didn't want him to know.

"That's okay," he said. "Seeing her riled brings out— Never mind." He chuckled. There must be *stuff* happening there this morning, too.

"I'll call her in a minute or so." She'd make sure BB knew this was all on her, not Joe. She hung up and turned off her phone. She'd talk to BB when she was ready, and not a moment before.

She stared at her reflection and took stock. Not bad. She was hardly dressed up fancy and her makeup was light as usual, but still, not bad. She took after her mom in the looks department. Good bones. Pretty hair that drew the eye, and the short shorts worked as a great distraction on recoveries.

She didn't wear them to expose herself. The purpose was to distract. Often, those few seconds were all that stood between her success and failure on a job.

In spite of failing to get the Morgan off the property, she counted today a success.

And if the heat in Mac's eyes was anything to judge by, she just might get more than she came for. Desire rose as she smoothed her hair, slicked on another swipe of lip gloss and stepped back out into the grandest entrance she'd ever seen.

Mac was sex on two legs and she was not about to deny him or herself. It might have been a while since she'd created thunder and lightning under the covers, but the way her morning was going, anything was possible.

Anything at all.

The murmur of male voices drew her around the staircase to join Mac and his head of security.

She'd already told them everything she knew. Truly, there was no reason to stay beyond Mac's and her mutual attraction. Braver than she'd ever been, she tested where she stood with Mac. "I don't know how much help I can be," she said as he watched her round the stairs. "I've already told you what I know."

If he agreed, or if his eyes had cooled in her absence, she'd wish him well and leave, no harm done.

MAC WATCHED MORGAN'S brows knit into a frown and fought the urge to smooth the line with the pad of his thumb. "I'd like you to stay," he said. Damn Jack and damn the stalker. He wanted her.

"You have a stalker?" she asked. Her concern touched him in places left cold by most women.

"I often do." He shrugged. Once it had been a porn actress who wanted to make the jump to Hollywood releases and figured she could cash in on a few photo ops with him, but Morgan didn't need to hear about that. "Comes with the territory. But usually it's just a misplaced crush. Someone gets hooked on the tabloid stories and wants to meet me."

"A crush?" She paled. "And this time it's different?"

"Seems to be." He tilted his head toward Jack barking

instructions into his phone. "We could move to the patio for a coffee and wait there for him to finish."

Her mouth widened in a smile that brimmed with relief, and sexual heat settled into her stance. "I'll just check in with BB." She dug into her satchel and pulled out a phone.

"BB?"

"The tracer slash office manager at Five Aces. She'll blow her stack when she finds out I'm here—I mean, still here. I'm usually much faster with recoveries." She hit a button, tapped her foot. "Hi, BB? Uh...you won't believe what happened." He heard a loud exclamation from the receiver. "Oh. You've seen Joe already." She walked back the way she'd come and leaned against the wall under the stairs. She snugged the phone close to her mouth. "Yes, I'm at his home right now. Yes, inside." Her voice went lower.

He hoped her job was safe. He'd never felt that particular concern himself. In his world people didn't have to worry about the next rent payment or food bill or medical expense, and it struck him that she could possibly have all those worries at once if she continued to buck the rules for him.

People made inconveniences go away for him. People made allowances and special arrangements for him. But he couldn't recall anyone ever making a sacrifice for him.

Morgan Swann had put a lot on the line. He wasn't sure how he felt about that, but the feelings roiled in his gut, a blend of respect, admiration and plain old desire. Toss in a twinge of humility because she was willing to put her job on the line for him, and Mac felt a serious case of like.

He *liked* her. Under her gruff get-the-job-done exterior

was a compassionate heart. She knew Mac was at a loss to explain the repossession orders. He needed time to get answers, and here she was, setting aside the rules on his behalf at a cost to herself.

She was one strange mixture and he wanted to know all he could about her.

If her decision to help them caused irreparable harm to her, he'd surrender the Morgan and deal with getting it back while Lindsay was on her honeymoon.

But if he surrendered the car right now, he might never see this woman again. That idea irked him.

Her shoulders hunched and it looked like she was being given a hard time by her manager. He wanted to rub her back, smooth her shoulders, take her burden, but that was way too much for her to accept at this point.

Jack flipped his phone closed. "The IT guys are on it. We'll know soon where the breach was and how it was done. What's the word from the bank?" He slanted an assessing glance at Morgan's back. "She having a hard time?"

"Looks like it. She's supposed to take the car in, regardless of what we say."

Jack nodded. "She's taken a leap of faith. A quick background check shows she's got no record, single, and has lived in the same place for years. Not a great neighborhood, but it's not the worst, either."

"So, she appears to be what and who she says she is?"

"Pretty much. But I'll look deeper if you see yourself spending more time with her." His gaze sharpened.

"I see myself spending as much time as it takes with her."

"As what takes?"

Mac rubbed his hand down his face to help sort out his feelings. "I'm not sure."

So far, Morgan's conversation with BB had been straight and to the point. "I'm telling you, this car has been paid for. There's some mistake, BB."

"Did I not tell you that something weird would happen on that estate?" BB let out a sigh but didn't wait for the *I told you so* to sink in before she went on. "The dealership was not paid. I don't know why and I don't care. Neither should you."

At least she'd stopped yelling about Morgan being inside the house. Even BB realized she wasn't in any physical danger. There wasn't a tire iron in sight. "You still expect me to bring in the Morgan?"

"You still want a job?"

An empty threat. BB wouldn't fire her, but her uncle might. BB was only two years older than Morgan, but at twenty-eight she already had a decade of experience in the business. Morgan bowed to that experience now. "All right, give me a couple of hours."

"Excuse me?"

"Mac's invited me for a coffee on the patio." Her belly heated with anticipation. Time alone with Mac. Her wildest fantasy come true. Out of her depth, she didn't quite catch BB's next question.

"Mac? Who's Mac?"

"What? Oh, Mac is Kingston. BB, he wants me to hang out with him. Alone." She didn't mean to sound giddy, but she couldn't help it. The feeling was familiar but ancient and, she'd hoped, long-buried.

She thought she'd learned her lesson back with Johnny DeLongo. She'd been a sucker and he'd all but destroyed her life.

The thrill felt the same, but Mac didn't want her to steal cars. He didn't want her anywhere but in his bed. Her belly fluttered in anticipation because she was half-way there.

"Morgan." BB's voice drew her attention. "Be careful. Don't let him go to your head."

"That's not where he's going."

"Oh, jeez. Be careful."

"I will. How much time can you give us? I mean, me?"

BB made her wait half a minute, while Morgan's nerves screeched at her to hurry. Mac was waiting. Finally, Morgan added, "His chief of security is looking into serious problems. Identity theft, computer hacking. They need time."

"And you want this time with McRae." She sighed. "Two hours." She disconnected.

BB must be in a good mood. She'd only threatened Morgan's job once. Morgan turned back to see the men deep in conversation near the door. Mac didn't seem worried, just attentive. Jack looked deadly serious.

Still out of her depth, the events that brought her here seemed stranger than ever. Maybe this was a dream.

She must have swapped work orders with Joe last night, then gone home and fantasized this whole scenario. Either that, or she'd fallen asleep under that over-grown bush across the road and she was about to wake up with a snort.

But her denim sack purse felt real as she curled her fingers into it. She curled her toes, too, and felt the warmth of her work socks. And her hands still smelled of the expensive scented soap from Mac's powder room.

The warmth in Mac's eyes was real. The welcome and

the interest were real, too. She melted at the sexy, smoky look he flashed her.

"Take care of it, Jack. Call me when things are back on track." His gaze darkened in intensity. Her panties moistened in response, while thrills of arousal danced low in her belly.

"What about tomorrow?" Jack asked.

"My orders on the wedding stand." Mac's voice was no-nonsense as he turned toward her. Jack backed off. He went up the stairs without another word, leaving Mac and Morgan alone in the front hall.

Excitement vibrated around her. Alone with Kingston McRae. She couldn't believe it. He took her breath when he focused intently on her. On *her!* Morgan Swann. She tried to convince herself she was dreaming, but what good was reality on a morning like this?

Reality could ruin a woman's good time. And Mac was promising a very good time.

"How did it go with your manager?"

She had to clear her throat. Words wouldn't come. Right, when she wanted to speak, her mutinous mouth failed her, but when she should be quiet, she blurted out rude questions. She tried again. "Two hours." She swiped her hand down her shorts onto her thighs. "But, whoa, was she angry."

"I'm grateful, Morgan." He reached for the hand at the top of her thigh and raised it to his lips. Reality slipped another notch as she watched him turn her palm up, only to dip his head to kiss her there. Tingles of awareness skittered down to her sex and back up to her heart. The moment stretched as he lingered over her palm.

She stood frozen, drinking the moment like honeyed tea.

Her heart thumped so hard she figured he could

hear it. "You have a wedding?" she squeaked. "Sorry, I couldn't help but overhear."

"Rory's granddaughter Lindsay is getting married. We need the car for the wedding." His eyes warmed with affection. "She's like a kid sister," he explained, and a wire that had been strung taut inside let go.

"Oh, that's nice. I like weddings." She'd been to seven of her mother's, but she still loved to hear the vows. Empty but pretty words for Elizabeth. Every time she heard her mother say them, Morgan made her own vow. If she ever chose to speak the words, every one would carry a lifetime of promise.

"That's why you bought the Plus 4. It has a back-seat." Very thoughtful. "It will make a beautiful wedding car."

"After the reception we'll take the bride and groom to the marina. I've offered them my yacht for a cruise. The groom has somewhere special in mind." His eyes focused on her mouth as he pulled her inexorably closer. She licked her lips, fascinated as his eyes flared into twin flames, enticing her to give in to the dream.

Her mind slipped into automatic as he lowered his head. Close. So close. His scent rose and mingled with her vanilla body lotion to blend into something spicy and erotic. She *was* dreaming!

Her world narrowed to Mac, his intentions, his need. Her own. She sighed and tilted her mouth upward. When she parted her lips, he took them softly, a test of her willingness. She slid into the kiss, let his mouth move on hers, tasting, coaxing.

He tasted of coffee and man and need.

She pressed against his mouth to move the kiss from tentative to definite. It may have been a while, but her body revved up in record time.

He lifted his mouth. "You taste like sunshine."

"You taste delicious."

"Will you be fired for asking for extra time?" His hips settled lightly against her lower body, his hands sat at the flare between her waist and hips. Such large, warm hands. The weight of them held her while his heat seeped through her cotton T-shirt to her skin and deeper, straight into her muscles.

"Not fired, but BB was angry. She knew I switched paperwork with one of the guys so I could come here this morning."

He frowned. "Why?"

"We don't get many calls on Mercer Island. I figured I'd get a peek at how the other half lives." She waved a hand at the foyer. "You do okay."

He laughed, hard. "You not only taste like sunshine, you bring it into this mausoleum. You threw open the door and breezed in."

He slid his hand down to hers and held it. Her arm tingled and she tried to wake herself, but why bother? Why ruin a perfectly good fantasy? Reality was never this good. "Let's go get some of Rory's coffee. I haven't had my full share today."

"Caffeine, elixir of the gods."

He led her into a massive kitchen at the back of the house with French doors that opened onto a patio and pool. Mac pulled out a stool for her at the granite-topped island. Then he poured her a steaming cup of French press coffee. Her first taste was heaven. "Mmm, did I say elixir?" When she put the cup down, he was looking at her from the far side of the island. She patted the stool beside her. "You could join me."

"You're safer if I stay over here."

She heated through to her core. "Oh."

He cleared his throat. "How much trouble will you be in at work?"

"I'll take care of it. It's Joe I'm more worried about. He's with BB now. He's taking the brunt of her lecture about drivers going places without her knowing."

"Joe's the man you switched with?"

She nodded.

"This Joe. Why would he do you that favor?" His gaze went sharp with the question.

She raised an eyebrow. "I promised to put in a good word for him with BB. He likes her, but she has a thing against dating the drivers. You may be surprised, but not all of them have always been upstanding citizens." She counted herself in that lineup, but it was too early in the conversation to mention it and she was already on shaky ground with Jack.

"Why's Jack so suspicious of me?"

"He's angry about some security breaches, and is hyperaware today. Your recovery of the Morgan is just another in a short series of strange events. You're the first person he can eyeball for anything. So you're at the forefront for suspicion."

"So, like, kill the messenger?"

"Something like that." Mac smiled. "Jack will liaise with BB. They'll sort it out in no time."

"Liaise? Sounds good." She drained her cup and set it gently on the countertop. She idly turned the cup between her fingers. "Jack and BB. Two pit bulls, one on the attack, the other on defense."

"Speaking of pit bulls, I admire your determination to get onto the grounds. You waited for hours across the street. Then picked your moment."

She warmed at the praise, but it was no more than

what she did on a daily basis. "People in the recovery business must be tenacious."

"And clever, too, I'd imagine." He reached across the counter and swept a tendril of hair from her cheek. Heat traced across her skin.

The tabloid stories hadn't done him justice. The clock ticking down the seconds seemed louder, more insistent. She couldn't let this chance slip away on small talk. Her interest in Mac had nothing to do with the *World Courier* stories and everything to do with the man himself. Her mind cleared. She wanted more than idle conversation.

She wanted this dream to segue into every fantasy of Kingston McRae she'd ever had. She remembered her decision to share quality time under the covers with a man.

"We have two hours," she whispered, thrilling at what she was about to say. "Let's make the best of them."

5

"I'M TRYING TO BE A gentleman, Morgan. If I walk around this island, I'll be anything but." He nailed her with his gaze as she straightened on the kitchen stool. "Think carefully. Are you sure?"

She glanced at the clock on the wall, heard the tick—louder, insistent. "One hour and fifty minutes. Time's wasting."

MAC NEEDED NO MORE encouragement as he stepped around the sandwich bar. Morgan flowed into his arms, as eager as he was. Her bottom filled his hands like melons warm from the sun. Her soft flesh brought him to full arousal. Civilized man dropped away as his inner cave dweller took over.

He kissed her, taking her mouth hard.

"If this is a dream," she whispered, "don't wake me till it's over."

He promised and kissed her again, molding her hips to his. Images flashed behind his eyes of Morgan as she'd stood up to him, to Jack, to her manager. Impressive. Lovely.

Her desire became an irresistible siren call to his

primal male. "Are you sure?" he asked again with the last coherent thought he had.

"Please, Mac. Yes."

She smiled, looking warm and pretty. Her lips were puffy from his kisses, the skin of her neck red with sexual flush. He trailed his hand down her slender arm and took her fingers to lead her to the foyer.

They took the stairs wrapped in each other, silent. Jack could emerge from the second-floor office at any moment. Rory could appear in the hall, efficient and curious.

He didn't want either man to see Morgan in this most private intimate state. This Morgan, this wanton, needful Morgan was for him alone.

He slid his hand from her waist to her buttock and gave her a light squeeze of appreciation. She was perfect, from her burnished auburn waves to those sexy, rolled-down work socks. When she squeezed his butt cheek, too, he almost howled with the need to hurry.

He took the lead and showed her into the master suite. As the door clicked shut, he pressed her against the wall, plundering her sweet mouth, seeking full surrender. The rush, the hard-driving lust shocked him speechless.

But he couldn't stop himself. Her scent, her need, her wild response drove him higher, harder, faster than any other woman. Between, kisses heated whispers sent steam up his spine to explode in his skull.

She smoothed her hands up his arms to his shoulders. "So much strength," she said before giving him her mouth again. She hitched her hips higher, closer to his erection. He lifted her so she could wrap her legs around his waist. Still not enough, not nearly enough.

His hands slipped up the back of her shorts to hold her naked flesh. His cock surged painfully.

Morgan moaned and undid his shirt buttons. "Need to touch you," she murmured, and swept her hands to his chest. "Oh, hair! I love hair." She finger-combed him, then found a nipple and drew it between her lips. His hips bucked in response.

"I'll lose it right now if you don't stop."

She took a deep breath and sighed. "You smell so good." Then she found his other nipple and teased it with gentle scrapes of her teeth.

Powerful urges to take—fast, hard—shocked him into stillness. The purely male need to complete the act paled in comparison to completing it with *this* woman. She was the one bringing him to his knees with want. He strained to hold back the tide. "Won't make it to the bed, Morgan." He pressed her back into the wall for support while he groped for his fly with one hand. His brain fogged as flames sparked in his lower spine.

She tipped her head back, her eyes ablaze with dark yearning. "Protection?"

That one word slowed him enough to carry her through his sitting room to the bed. He set her on her feet on the mattress, and put his face to her chest. He bowed his head and drew in air while his heart pounded in time to the thudding of hers.

"It's been a while for me," she said. "I don't do this kind of thing."

"I don't want to hurt you by going too fast." But he wanted to plunder and take. Wanted to bury himself inside her. This floundering made no sense, but all he could do was ride it out. See where it led.

With her? a whisper came. *Why not her?*

His breathing slowed, control returned. He nuzzled her breasts and sucked in her scent while she pulled off her T-shirt.

Her cleavage was spectacular. He tugged the bra's half cups down to see her nipples. Her breasts were high, round and tipped with dark rose areolae. She clasped his head and brought his mouth to her. He caught the tip of one breast and sucked strongly. Her knees buckled and he held her up with one hand.

He palmed her thigh with the other and slid his fingers up, up, up to her core. Her wonderful, sexy, alluring short shorts gave up her secrets in a heartbeat as his fingertip found her wet center. She moaned and creamed moisture onto his finger at first touch. So responsive, so needy.

"This is crazy, but I trust you, Mac." Her eyelids drooped and he let her sag to the mattress. Her boots dangled over the edge.

"These boots," he said. "You want to talk crazy? These things turning me on is crazy." He lifted both feet and placed them on the bed, then opened her legs to accommodate the breadth of his shoulders.

Her soft inner thighs filled his vision. She slipped her hands down to cover the narrow denim crotch.

"You're so lovely, Morgan. May I look? Please?"

THE HANDSOME PLAYBOY wanted permission? Morgan held her breath to keep her head from spinning. She slid her palms to her thighs to give him the view he begged for.

Using one fingertip, he drew soft circles on her inner thigh, close to her needy flesh. She moaned and moved her hips but he did no more than bless the inside of her knee with a kiss.

She shuddered at his tenderness. "Please, Mac. Touch me." His shoulders braced her legs open, leaving her vulnerable. But oaken flames danced in the depths of his gaze while he ran his hands to her bottom and tugged off her shorts.

Surreal eroticism kept her spellbound. This was Kingston McRae...*no*...this was Mac and she wanted him as much as he wanted her.

Moist heat bloomed between her legs.

And he knew it. She could see that in his eyes.

Most men would have been on her, in her before she had a chance to catch her breath. The man she might have met to ease her loneliness for a night wouldn't care to please her, wouldn't ease her slowly into bed, making sure that she was with him one hundred percent.

But Mac, her personal dream weaver, drove her mad with his patience. "There's no hurrying you, is there?"

Filtered light from floor-to-ceiling windows bathed the bed in a warm glow while Mac tugged at her boot laces. "You're wearing lace underwear and scuffed leather work boots. It's not a combination I've seen before. I like it." He tugged again and got nowhere with the stubborn lace.

"I double-knot my laces. Sorry."

"It's either slow down long enough to do this or rip the crotch out of your shorts."

It was on the tip of her tongue to vote for tearing her shorts when he found the tightest loop and pulled the lace free. He set to work on the second boot.

"Want some help with this one?" she offered, but he'd already undone the lace. The second boot joined the first on the floor.

"Now," he said as he stood and towered over the bed. He was so large, so powerful: physically, mentally and emotionally. "Let's get naked," he said. He shucked his slacks and tore off his shirt, while she slipped out of her bra, shorts and panties.

When she reached to tug off her socks, he stayed her hand. "Leave those on. Good God, Morgan, you're sexy as hell and those socks, rolled down just that way at the end of your gorgeous legs, are about to put me over the top."

She chuckled, glowing at the compliments. Silly what could turn a man on, but who was she to argue? She'd spent seven years lusting for this man in grainy newsprint photos.

And now, here she was, living the dream.

He stood ready, flushed, muscle and sinew taut with need and aimed straight at her.

Hallelujah.

The hair that she'd nuzzled earlier spread across the expanse of his chest, then narrowed as it crossed his flat belly. It bloomed, darker and thicker, at his groin.

His penis rose toward her, and she melted at his obvious control, needing to hold him close.

Hold him in the crux of her body, her arms and legs entwined with his. She wanted to feel his hips bearing down, his chest heavy and hard on hers, the scent of his heated neck, the caress of his silky hair when she nuzzled his ear.

She wanted him in the fullest way a woman could want a man.

Kneeling on the bed, she trailed her nose along his clavicle, drinking in the aroused scent of him. She cupped his sac and let her fingers play his shaft. His hips arched toward her in silent need.

He groaned, then took her to the mattress with him. She sank into the bedding, legs flared, knees bent, skin to skin, heartbeat to heartbeat as he took his position between her thighs.

She kissed him eagerly in welcome.

A sigh, a moan, a kiss with deep tongue strokes and— The sound of the packet opening gave her a wary moment.

This was happening. Now. Here. And he was huge!

She held his arms and pressed herself up so he'd slow and look at her. Momentous expectation filled his gaze. "Please?"

"I like you, Mac. I think you're a good man." She believed it. "A dream weaver."

He hesitated. "Thank you." The warmth in his gaze deepened as he believed it, too.

Then he slipped his hand to her bottom, held her hips up and slid into her in one smooth motion. She took him in, opening to receive him fully.

"You're so wet. So hot." He pulled out, drawing each silken muscle taut. Her channel clasped him as she gasped with the exquisite sensation.

"Oh, Mac! This is…you are…" Words failed as she succumbed to the tension of his slow, easy rhythm.

He brushed hair from her face. His eyes burned with each plunge and retreat as he stretched and filled her. He changed tempo and pumped faster, pressing deeper with each stroke until she crowned and burst into a pulsing release.

She groaned and grabbed him tight, urging him on until he, too, lost control.

A guttural groan rumbled around her with his release. The pulsing that filled her channel was not her own as he tensed and stilled in her arms.

She held him close, anchoring him while he shook against her, his heart slowing with hers.

He surprised her by rolling to his back, carrying her with him. Content to let him hold her, she sprawled across his big body.

"I love your chest, the scent of your skin." She sounded almost reverent with the afterglow. "This was the best time I've ever had."

He chuckled. "I'm glad." He weaved his fingers through her hair. "I love your hair. It's like silk." His other hand slid to her bottom. "And I love your ass. You wear those hot shorts to distract men."

She grinned into his chest. "Of course not." But her shaking shoulders gave away the lie. "Okay, okay, you caught me. I figure if the guy's checking out my Daisy Dukes then he might not catch on to what I'm doing in time to stop me." She lifted her head to find his eyes full of mischief. "You'd be surprised how effective that is."

He kissed the tip of her nose. "Your butt was a major distraction for me. I couldn't think when I stepped out the door and saw you bent over so prettily."

"And then you saw my socks?"

"Ah! Your socks cinched the deal." He laughed and rubbed his feet against hers, hooking his big toe in the woolly folds at her ankles. He growled, making her giggle, then tapped her bottom for permission to rise. She slid off, feeling generous and affectionate.

His stroke on her cheek spoke of similar feelings. Maybe it was the sex, but she preferred to think it was more than that.

He strode into the master bath and shut the door, leaving her to gather her thoughts. If nothing else, maybe they could part as friends.

It was a nice thought. Appealing under the circumstances. In spite of her decision to seek quality adult time, she probably wouldn't have gone through with the plan. A guy she chose for a one-night stand would have to be outstanding. Irresistible.

Like Mac. He'd charmed her so thoroughly and

completely, she'd let down her guard. Perhaps she
shouldn't have given in to her dreams and fantasies this
last hour, but she couldn't be sorry.

She closed her eyes, determined to hold on to the
dream of Kingston McRae for as long as she could.

If he walked out of the bathroom and looked cold or
dismissive, she'd dress and leave before he said anything
to wound her. That way, she could walk away with sweet
memories and sweeter dreams.

From the sounds in the bathroom, she wouldn't have
time to dress, so she did the next best thing and wrapped
herself in the sheet. She stood by the window.

Life with her mother had taught her that a woman
should depend on herself. Morgan never expected or
wanted a man to rescue her. Her happiness and security
was up to her. Johnny DeLongo had taught her that lesson
so well she'd never forgotten it. Would never forget it.

She could still see Elizabeth telling the judge that
Morgan should go to Juvenile Hall, that it would do her
good. Elizabeth had wanted the time to find husband
number four. Or was that five?

Thank God the judge had come up with a different so-
lution. Morgan had been sent to a halfway house famous
for turning kids with potential around. The counselors
had offered her a chance to prove her talents, to see she
was a capable person in her own right. She had no idea
where she'd be if she hadn't been given that break.

Clouds had rolled in while they'd been making love.
The light had softened to muted gray. Seattle in June.

The window overlooked the back of the estate. In the
distance, against the stone wall that enclosed the grounds,
stood a garden shed. In the middle of the grounds was
a huge maple tree that had to have been old when Mac

was a boy. In the summer the shade under the tree would be deep and cool.

She studied the images to keep for future dreams. Her fantasy life would be enriched by the details she could pull up.

Directly below the window a hot tub sat beside a kidney-shaped pool. The flagstone patio showed its age. Some of the stones had shifted.

The back garden brought Mac into a new light, a realistic one. He was a guy whose house needed upkeep. He'd already renovated the kitchen for Rory's sake, but this mansion was wasted on a pair of bachelors.

The Kingston McRae she'd fantasized about didn't exist. That man had been manufactured by the tabloids and embellished to near-royal status by her lonely, overactive imagination.

If she wasn't careful, a full-out infatuation would take her down.

Mac came to stand behind her, his hands on her upper arms and his chin by her ear. He'd been so gentle with her, leashing his power.

"Sorry, did I catch you unawares?" He spoke into her ear, then added a kiss and a nibble on her neck. She tilted to give him access.

"I was wondering what the hell I'm doing here. Aside from the obvious, of course."

He gathered her close. One sly hand slipped under the sheet and cupped her mound. "The obvious is enough for now, isn't it?"

"Yes," she said as moisture gathered where he rubbed her with delicate ease. "Oh, that feels good."

"So wet. So warm." He pulled her backside close to align with his rising cock.

"Again?" she whispered.

He kissed her neck, then moved down to her shoulder, nipping her. "Sorry to be so obvious. And I'm especially sorry that I'm rushing you, but—"

He rubbed her clitoris, using her own wetness to ease the friction. She arched her back toward him and opened her legs for more. "I can't get enough of you, Morgan. You surprise and delight me."

She whirled, dropping the sheet. Naked, she pressed her hands to his shoulders. This time, she had to keep it real. "I'm twenty-six, Mac, long past the need for declarations. This is what it is. A couple of stolen hours."

Hours that would live forever in her dreams.

She pushed harder and walked him backward two steps. Three.

He grinned as her intent became clear. When the back of his legs hit the bed, she shoved hard enough to tumble them both.

She straddled him. "I want to make the most of our time, then I'll leave." To prove her point, she raised her hips, took his hand and slid it to her honeyed center. "See? I'm more than ready."

He found her clitoris, ripe and firm as a new plum. He slid a finger deep inside her but it wasn't enough. "Clever man," she said when she saw a fresh condom packet on the bed. She tore it open and settled at his side to roll it down his shaft.

He raised her face with a finger and his expression softened. "I was right about you."

"How?"

"There's not a coy bone in your body. You know what you want and you get it."

"Always." She warmed at the admiration in his voice. "And what I want right now is you." The first time with Mac might have been a dream, but this was as real as sex could get. They were healthy, normal *available* people, free to spend time with each other if they chose.

That it would be the only time didn't diminish her enjoyment in the least. She slid her fingers along his jaw, memorizing the feel of his stubble, his strength, the warmth of his skin.

Suddenly a man's voice sounded in the hall outside the bedroom door. Rory.

"No, I can't say where he's got to."

Mac covered her hand to still her exploration. "Damn it. He'll knock any second."

She closed her eyes with a sigh. Just as well, Mac had gotten to her. Better to cut it off quick.

"Morgan, we'll finish this. We will." He cursed. "Just give me half an hour." He rose and bussed her firmly on the lips.

The expected knock came and she nodded at him. "Sure. But, um, could I ask for one favor?"

He slipped into his slacks. "Of course." He clasped her chin in his hands and kissed her deeply.

"Could you let me know how this all pans out? If you catch your stalker?"

"You mean when."

"It's okay if it's just a message. Jack could leave it with BB for me."

He narrowed his gaze. "You're taking off as soon as I walk out."

"I don't wait well. Too impulsive, I guess." He didn't need to know that her mother had begged for the attention of the men in her life. Morgan refused to live that way.

He straightened and ignored Rory's second knock. "You'd go back on your word that we'd have two full hours?"

That was exactly what she'd planned. But when his frown deepened she couldn't disappoint him or herself. "There's forty-five minutes left, then I'm gone."

The side of his mouth kicked up and he kissed her again. This time, he fondled her breast and groaned. "Don't leave, Morgan. Please."

"I won't."

He studied her face for a long moment before he released her. "I believe you. If it was anyone else, I wouldn't."

"Go, before Jack and Rory barge in. They may think you're kinky when they see I still have my socks on."

"I wouldn't leave you on any other day, you know that, right?"

"If any other man said that, I wouldn't believe him. Now, go find out what Jack's learned. Maybe the whole repo thing has been cleared up and you can keep the car." She didn't want to ruin the wedding, but he could use a limo. Surely he had a couple.

"Every kiss makes me want more," he said, and looked startled at his own statement.

When he walked out, her fingers stayed on her quivering lips, holding in the taste of him, the feel of his determined kiss. Did he really feel the same way she did?

That couldn't be right. She was the one with the infatuation. Not him. Not Mac McRae.

When the door to the suite opened, she heard Jack's voice. "We've got something, Mac. This is probably a woman…someone you've dated."

An ex! Of course. Lots of exes got possessive and weird. The news was full of the violence of scorned lovers. She shouldn't stick her nose into their discussions. This wasn't her business.

This time, she had to stay on the sidelines.

She squelched an impulsive urge to charge out into the hall to help.

Oh! To hell with it. She had to know, had to offer her help if Mac needed it.

She slammed back into her clothes, making sure her T-shirt was on right side out, and marched toward the door.

6

RORY AND JACK WERE in the hall when Mac stepped out.

"Check that the garden shed's secure," Jack told Rory.

"You should have let me cover that door years ago." Rory looked to Mac.

"It still comes in handy on occasion," Mac said. Both his parents had used the secret entrance. Her mother, for liquor deliveries, his father as an escape route to rendezvous with women he wouldn't be seen with in public.

Rory's expression was bland as he headed down the hall, while Jack's was condemning. "This Morgan could be setting you up for anything." Jack rounded on Mac. "A paternity suit or assault charges. You don't know the first thing about her, and—"

"I know enough." He was usually more cautious, but he was sick of caution. Beyond the physical, Morgan touched him in ways he couldn't describe.

Jack scoffed. Mac didn't wait for his next comment but led the way into his office and took his position by the window, his mind still on Morgan. The reflection showed Jack's concerned expression and prematurely gray head.

The whole team ragged the security chief about his early silver, Mac included. Idly Mac wondered if the gray affected his success with women, but he doubted it. Jack never complained.

"We've narrowed the list of personal suspects to Maria Sandoval, Gretchen Eriksen and Lila Markham."

"And the business-related suspects?"

"Much longer. People hate you for your success, Mac. You cost a lot of people their jobs over the years and this recession—"

"None of the businesses I turned around have ever asked for bailouts. And bonuses are the first thing to go when I take over."

"Which plays well with the public, but those disappearing bonuses are important to some people."

Mac nodded but remained unconvinced. This had the feel of a prank more than a serious threat.

"What about the women, Mac?"

"I dated them," he said with a nod. "So what? They were mostly set up by our PR people. For convenience. For their careers, not mine." He hoped Morgan hadn't misconstrued his rush out of the bedroom.

"Mac?" Jack's stern voice pulled him back. "Get your head in the game. No cause for a broken heart for any of them?"

"I don't think so." He pulled up what he remembered of Maria Sandoval. "Maria is an actress, ambitious to a fault." She was eager to start her own line of gym wear. "You remember she asked me to appear in an infomercial wearing her workout clothes."

Jack snorted. "Not likely. I can't see you in fuchsia tights."

"Exactly. When I learned she'd used my name to get financial backing, I said goodbye." Being used was par for the course, but Maria had been underhanded. If she'd asked him, he might have provided her with the money she wanted, but by going behind his back, she'd lost his trust.

"Didn't her manager get an ex-rapper involved?"

"Strictly C-list. He'd discovered bodybuilding after his music career tanked and thought the infomercial would reignite interest."

Morgan showed up in the window's reflection, framed by the doorway. "I remember him," she said clearly. "He was sent to prison for three months and came out buff. I think he discovered steroids behind bars."

Mac faced her with a private smile, happy she hadn't cut and run. "Morgan, glad you could join us."

Jack, decidedly, was not. He faced her, too, his back stiff and shoulders squared. Jack could freeze a Caribbean island with his stare and Morgan's reaction proved it.

Her eyes widened, then unbelievably she faltered and hung back by the door, indecision carved into her beautiful face.

"How do you know so much about this rapper?" Jack demanded.

"I read about him," she responded softly. "I have a memory for things I read. I'm better at that than remembering what I hear, so I get my news from papers."

"So you read the *World Courier?*" Jack barked. "Maybe you've been caught up in all the stories about Mac?"

She paled and opened her mouth to speak, but closed it again.

"Don't be ridiculous, Jack," Mac cut in. "I told you Morgan's not my stalker." He hadn't expected her to join them, but now that she was here, he saw a way for her to help. "But, Morgan, if you read tabloids, maybe you can remember details we've missed. Can you recall anything about Gretchen Eriksen?"

Mac drew her into the room. Her confidence restored, she raised an eyebrow at Jack as she passed him. Mac didn't relax until she took a seat in front of his desk.

"Gretchen Eriksen," Morgan said. "Tall, natural blonde, she's been in a lot of rehabs lately." She shrugged. "Can't seem to stick to it, I guess."

Mac nodded. "That's her."

"Pfft! I can't believe you ever went out with her," she said. Her pert nose wrinkled. "What did you see in her anyway?"

Jack's eyebrows rose, but he shut his mouth at a look from Mac.

"I escorted her a couple of times as a favor to my PR guy." Gretchen's rapid-fire conversation and wild eyes made him suspect drug use. He'd cut her off quickly when she wanted to spend the night. Perhaps she'd felt snubbed, but since he hadn't gone on more than a couple of photo-op dates with her, she didn't seem a likely suspect. He said as much.

Jack disagreed. "She's erratic. She might be the one. I'll check her out."

"Scratch Lila Markham off the list," Mac said. "She's recently engaged to the actor who was in that popular fantasy flick a couple months ago." She'd moved on quickly after the flame of attraction had died. He hadn't looked back and neither had she. When her engagement was announced he'd sent his congratulations.

Morgan supplied Lila's fiancé's name and the month of the upcoming nuptials. She squirmed in her seat. "Lila's trying to keep the details of the wedding private, but information's leaking out. It'll be big and flashy."

When she saw Jack watching her with consternation on his face, she eased back on her enthusiasm for reporting what she'd read. "That was, um, last Thursday's edition." She cleared her throat.

Jack slanted her a wicked glance, as if she'd just confirmed his suspicions. To Mac he said, "You scratch Lila off *your* list. I won't."

"Can you recall anything else you've read, Morgan?" Mac asked.

"You dated these women in the last year. With about a month in between each one."

Jack glared at Mac. For Morgan to have such detailed knowledge, she must have read every story they'd planted. Mac caught her eye and held it. "You and I have to talk about the pap I've fed the public."

"Okay," she said, "but it's clear you're not the man in the tabloid stories. You're more than that. At least to me." She blinked and gave him the sweetest smile. He thought he'd seen every expression in her arsenal, but that open look of affection nearly brought him to his knees.

His cock twitched as their mutual look heated.

Jack stood and broke the tension. "How much tabloid reading did you say you do?"

Mac stepped in to deflect the question. "None of these women seem like suspects to me. Collectively they're ambitious, and they have varying degrees of talent. Individually they're too busy with their own careers to focus on me."

Jack agreed. "To compromise the security monitors would require access to the house, and none of them has been here in months."

"And neither have I," Mac reminded him. "But Rory will know if there's been a maintenance crew around in recent days."

Jack left to hunt Rory down and Mac moved to Morgan's side, anxious to renegotiate the remaining time. "They're going to be back right away and we're down to thirty minutes."

She flushed and rose to kiss him. Her breasts brushed against his shirt and her nipples pebbled prettily. He slipped his arms around her and held her warm bottom.

"I want you to stay for the day," he said.

"So Jack will have enough time to run a background check on me?"

"I want to know more about you." He put up his hand to stop her protest. "Not in the way Jack does. No matter what I say, he's going to run his checks. I want to know you, Morgan. You intrigue me."

"I can't imagine why." She smiled, and desire started a burn as his blood rushed south.

"We were interrupted. I'd like to make it up to you."

"I'd like that, too."

Before he could do more than kiss her, Jack returned. His edgy stance made Morgan blink. "I noticed a great soaker tub," she said. "Mind if I indulge?"

"I'll take you back to the suite."

"No, Jack needs you. I don't want to interfere. I'll manage."

He told her where to find fresh towels and perfume for the bath and watched her go, sorry he couldn't join her.

"You've lost your frigging mind." Jack glared at him, frustration burning. "Or your mind's *on* frigging. Either way, Mac, you gotta get your head back in the game."

Mac had expected the blast, just not the intensity.

Jack glanced at the door Morgan had just exited. "Why her? She's nothing like the women you date. She wears combat boots and leather work gloves. What the hell are you thinking?"

Mac shrugged, held up his palms. "That she's nothing like the other women I've dated." He nodded, slowly, to keep Jack from guessing that he had envisioned her, naked and wet, in his built-for-two soaker tub. "And you, my friend, do not imagine her in those boots. You don't think about those gloves, either on or off. Get me?"

Jack put his hands up in surrender. "Fine, you just keep your head."

"You're right. I'm intrigued by Morgan, more than I've ever been intrigued by a woman before." His interest would burn out, but until then, he saw no reason to condone Jack's comments. "Now, butt out."

Jack's terse nod was the only agreement he'd get. It would have to do.

"Rory checked with the bank," Jack said. "The payment came out of your account, but the dealership says it's not showing at their end."

Mac nodded. "Then, sometime after I left for Africa, the dealership's accounting program was hacked into and the account changed to show it unpaid." He continued. "So their accounts would be out by the payment amount."

"If they left the money floating in the dealership's system, and didn't steal it, it's more proof this is all about you. Hell, they could have wiped out your bank account while they were at it. This is a taunt, a warning, a game," Jack said. His frustration tinged every word.

"I'd like to know what the point of this game is," Mac said. "And who hates me this much."

"And what's the prize for the winner?" Jack added.

The picture was almost perfect now. The infant—if all went well, a girl—smiled from a bassinet. A click of the mouse and the baby's cheeks turned a lovely shade of pink. Another click and the image printed.

She sighed. Mac would love a daughter. A little princess with oak-leaf eyes and light brown hair. Maybe some highlights. For a girl, highlights would be a must. And she'd be pretty, with even white teeth and a lovely thin body. Long limbs.

Perfection.

But perfection would only be achieved if he came to his senses. If he realized what he'd walked away from.

She had a mere handful of good breeding years left. If he waited much longer, she'd run the risk of needing help to conceive. She didn't want rounds of therapy. She'd had enough of doctors to last a lifetime. Mac had to know she would be the perfect mother and that her child by him would be the same.

She smoothed her hair, checked her reflection in the mirror over the desk. Every man wanted perfection.

Kingston McRae was no exception.

Content with the baby's image, she trimmed the photo then slipped it into the album. Another goal accomplished.

Visualization, that's what her therapist had said. Visualize and it will happen. She closed the cover, smoothed her fingers over the pretty pink satin.

Her coffee cooled at her elbow. Hotel coffee. Not as good as the French press she'd taken to Mac's. He'd liked it. She knew he had, although he'd never said.

Rory probably took credit for bringing it into the house. *Rory!* Anger ripped through her, silent yet violent.

She didn't like it when her hands shook; they gave too much away. She stared at them until she controlled the tremors. She would only free the rage if she had no choice. If *Mac* gave her no choice.

If he didn't understand her warnings, further steps would have to be taken.

Lindsay planned to use Mac's yacht for her honeymoon. A pity to have it impounded for unpaid slip fees, but Lindsay would get over the disappointment, and the embarrassment to Mac would soon fade. Lindsay deserved the inconvenience for not maintaining their friendship.

She should have been a bridesmaid, but Lindsay hadn't asked. That particular disappointment had cut, but the ruined honeymoon would more than make up for it.

No real harm done. Definitely in the forgivable realm of actions taken.

Mac would forgive her once he saw the glory of their reunion and her plans for their life together.

Going up against him and Jack Carling had been easier than expected. Hacking into the car dealership and her plan to ruin the honeymoon easier still.

She opened the closet to try on her dress for the wedding tomorrow. With a new hair color and style and lifts in her shoes, he wouldn't recognize her. In the morning, she'd complete her disguise by adding width to her nose and drawing in slightly heavier brows. She missed her hair extensions but the new cut was radically different. All in all, an asset.

She'd make certain he saw her from a distance. She'd dance with every other man there. Yes, Mac would look, but not touch. She would be unapproachable, out of bounds, and Mac would respond.

She refused to fawn over him. Always had.

She'd follow up with a brief personal visit to his estate. A few days after the wedding seemed appropriate. Mac would be thinking fondly of family and commitment.

And he would find those things with her. Or there would be regrettable consequences. Most regrettable.

The red satin complemented her pale skin and brought color to her face. Quite natural, she thought, considering she was usually a redhead.

AFTER HER BATH, Morgan dressed and stepped out into the hall. Mac was in the foyer below. He looked up at her, his face breathtakingly handsome and alight with male interest. A stab of regret reminded her that her fantasy was over. "I'm ready to go. And just under the two-hour limit, too. Not bad." She kept her tone breezy, refusing to let him see her falter.

"Join me on the patio for lunch. Jack called BB and she's not expecting you back."

She halted five steps from the bottom. "Really? She gave us more time?"

"Yes."

"You'll have to explain this—it's hard to believe. BB's a stickler."

When they headed out to the patio and she took a seat, he said, "I think Jack's willing to stop looking at you as if you're a walking detonator."

"I doubt I've completely passed muster, though. He probably assumes I'm a gold digger, or worse." She couldn't blame him considering the odd way they'd all met.

"After talking to Jack, your BB called the dealership and they've agreed to give us the weekend to sort through our security breaches. I gave them a substantial deposit pending the outcome of the investigation, of course."

The tabloids would have a field day if they caught wind of a recovery on the estate. Kingston McRae in financial trouble? They'd gobble the story up and spit him out on the sidewalk without a care for the truth.

"So that's why BB eased off." That, and BB had a way of getting to the bottom of things. "I'm glad you'll have the Morgan for the wedding. How many breaches have you had? Maybe Jack's right to be concerned for your safety."

He counted off on his fingers. "The monitors, the gates, the car payment. And a couple of other odd things that Jack considers warnings."

"This seems like an insider to me. Someone knows passwords, account numbers and security codes." A shiver ran down her spine. Someone close to Mac, someone who knew the real man, had done these things. But to what end?

As head of Mac's security, Jack had to put Morgan's presence in the liability column. "It's no wonder Jack's suspicious of me, but I think he should be looking closer to home." Mac had told her Lindsay was like a sister to him, but she hadn't met her yet. "I guess Lindsay's busy with last-minute wedding details?"

"Since six this morning. She's run off her feet."

"Any of her girlfriends develop crushes on you?" At the word "crushes" she felt a wave of heat in her face. But her crush had been impossibly distant. A friend of Lindsay's might have had higher hopes.

He shook his head. "Lindsay's been careful in her friendships, and with her busy schedule, it's been years since the house was invaded by girls." He shuddered. "But in her teens, she was as exuberant as any other teenager. Nothing serious, but Rory tore his hair out on occasion."

His affection for Rory and Lindsay was clear and she envied the easiness of their relationship. She and her mother were often prickly with each other. Morgan's teens had been much worse than prickly.

"As far as the monitors go, Rory was bamboozled into allowing an *employee* onto the grounds to check the system. The security company we use was sold last year. They swear they advised their clients by letter, but Rory never received one. He checked."

"Was the letter stolen?"

He shrugged. "Could have been. The mailbox is outside the gate. Whoever this is planned ahead."

"You haven't said much about your parents." They were still alive. She'd never read anything about their deaths. "Could this be directed at them?"

"They live as far apart as they can, although they both see this place as the family home. They visit but never at the same time."

From what she recalled, they had divorced quite civilly years ago. Old money was like that, she figured, unwilling to air their dirty linen or expose their reputations to ridicule. Unlike Elizabeth, who always made a lot of noise when it came to divorce. The squeaky wheel syndrome. The more she squeaked about private things, the more likely she was to be paid to go away quietly.

Rory stepped out onto the patio to tell Mac there was a call for him. He excused himself and Morgan called BB to check in.

"Morgan, what's going on?" her friend demanded. Her voice was low and heated. "And have you lost your mind?"

"Apparently, I have," she said, considering that in the last eighteen hours she'd behaved in ways she never had before—completely off the charts.

Which BB was spending considerable time ragging

her about. "And who's this Jack Carling? He called here to question me."

Which launched another string of questions and answers. Morgan didn't mind. BB needed to know what had happened so she could report to her uncle.

But it seemed Jack's calls had been relentless as he'd tracked down leads, starting with Five Aces. "I have to give the guy credit. He's good and knows how to get information from people without them realizing." Morgan heard a grudging respect for the security head in BB's voice. "What's he look like?"

Morgan chuckled. "Jack's a silver fox. Prematurely gray, which on him is pretty damn hot. He's got great shoulders. And is only an inch shorter than Mac." Maybe she should think of him as a silver wolf. "Also, he's protective of Mac. They go back a long way."

"Speaking of Mac, what's happening with him? And you?"

She heated at the question. "It's crazy, but I think he likes me." Filling BB in on everything but the rocket-blazing sex went quickly.

"You be careful, Morgan. These things have a way of burning out faster than you think they will. The stronger the blaze the faster the end comes."

She closed her eyes and pressed the phone tighter to her ear. "I know, BB. I'm being careful, but this is like the wildest dream come true." But her decision to keep it real had helped ground her.

"Keep your head on straight." There was a long pause and Morgan waited for a lecture. But in the end, BB just clicked her tongue as if there was nothing to be gained by saying more. "Call me when you leave. I want to know all the details. There's a lot you haven't said." She sighed. "I told you something weird would happen there. I knew it!"

"This is weird, but in a good way. Honest." She saw Rory open the slider. "Lunch is on the way, I've got to go." They said goodbye and she turned off her phone, setting it on the table.

Rory must be feeling the stress. He wasn't a young man. Instead of the tuxedo, he'd slipped into comfortable cords, a polo shirt and loafers. She jumped up to close the slider behind him. Taking the tray when he had it gripped firmly in both hands would be tricky, especially with the uneven flagstones. "Watch your step here, Rory."

He slanted her an amused glance. "I'm not senile, or unsteady on my feet, Morgan. This stone's been uneven for twenty years. I'd fall on my face if it ever got fixed!"

His humor helped her relax. He wasn't as stuffy as he'd first seemed in his tuxedo. In fact he was friendly and had a twinkle in his eye that hinted he'd once been a Romeo. She liked him, and oddly enough, he seemed to have taken to her, too.

A warmth traveled down her spine as Mac settled both hands on her shoulder and started a light massage. "Where did you come from?" she asked, startled.

"The den's beside the kitchen. Every room on this floor has a door out here."

She looked over her shoulder and counted. Sure enough. Four sets of doors altogether. He slipped into the chair across from her.

"This looks great, Rory, thanks," he said.

"I managed BLTs," Rory said, "but you're on your own if you need anything more substantial."

Mac leaned forward and waggled his eyebrows at her. "Rory makes the best BLTs you've ever tasted."

"I've tasted my share of good ones," she said as Rory slipped croissant sandwiches and bottled spring water onto the teak patio table, "but none that looked as delicious as this." He adjusted the overhead umbrella to give them coverage if the clouds broke.

"I'm heading out to meet Lindsay, then on to the rehearsal and then the dinner," Rory said. "I'll see you in the morning." The twinkle in his eye blazed with humor. He gave her a wink before he turned briskly and left.

"You're buddies," she said as she picked up one half of the sandwich.

"Rory's like a father to me. And Lindsay's the younger sister I didn't have."

"I saw two heavy, black leather loungers in front of the flat-screen television in the den. I like that you two hang out."

"I even tolerate his old war movies."

"You don't have to introduce me to Lindsay if it'll be awkward for you. I'm not the type of woman you usually date. Just ask Jack," she teased. In her mind there was no doubt that she'd stay the night. No question that they would make the most of their opportunity for more stupendous sex.

She couldn't remember when or if she'd ever been this satisfied and this horny at the same time.

"I'll be happy to introduce you." The gleam of deep affection in his gaze convinced her of it. For the first time, she wondered if there could be more to this day. At least more time, if not a greater emotional connection. But he had the wedding tomorrow and all the distractions of his investigation. She didn't want to pressure him.

While they ate, the talk turned small and comfortable. She learned that Rory was Navy, which explained his bearing.

"I like him," she said. "He's efficient but not stuffy. When I saw him in his tux I wondered what I'd stepped into."

Mac polished off his sandwich. "He agreed to wear one for the wedding." Amusement rang through his words. "And, for what it's worth, he likes you, too. I can tell."

Having Rory's approval warmed her.

"You've impressed Jack, too, although I'm not certain that extends as far as liking you."

"I can live with that." Not that it mattered much. This might stretch into a week or two, but the lust would be slaked, the attraction would fall away and she'd be yesterday's woman. "Jack's kind of impressive himself, but I'll reserve judgment on whether I like him or not."

He raised his brow. "Careful, lady, you're treading on shaky ground. Jack and I go way back. I know how many women he's left behind."

She gave him her best teasing smile, then moved to a safe topic. The evening had closed in and she let the peace of the gardens and the gentle undulation of the water in the pool ease through her. "It's so lovely here, peaceful."

"Your home is not a refuge?"

She huffed. "Don't pretend Jack didn't do a search on me. You know where I live." Her building was comfortably affordable and she had the smallest unit there. Cheap rent meant she could donate money regularly to the youth center that meant so much to the neighborhood.

She wondered how far back they could and would check. "So will Jack do a *complete* background check on me?"

"Not unless I tell him to." He seemed surprised at the

question. For him and his millionaire buddies, background checks were probably an everyday occurrence.

"And when do you decide to do that?"

"When I've decided to see more of a woman."

"Oh." If she'd pegged Jack Carling correctly, he was deep into the search already, regardless if Mac had asked or not.

"And I want to see more of you, Morgan."

The admission shouldn't have stunned her as much as it did. Rather than cooling off with the down-to-earth concerns of the worrisome day, their attraction still blazed and their mutual interest was higher than ever. As much as it pained her to confess her past difficulties with the law, she wanted him to remember her as someone who told him the truth. Since the day the judge had given her a break, she'd done her utmost to live honestly. "There's something you should know."

Why was this so tough? She usually shared her past easily. The kids at the youth center knew, the other drivers knew. But with Mac, it would be a wrench if the light in his eyes went out when he looked at her. Still, she couldn't go any further without being up-front. And to do that she had to go way back.

"Stepdad number four came with a couple of muscle cars. I was about eleven when he showed up. Anyway, I fell in love with cars and he taught me a lot, including how to drive years before I was legal." She took a deep breath. "I, um, eventually stole a few."

"Joyriding." He waved a hand in dismissal. "A rite of passage. I took my dad's Jag to California one weekend when I was fifteen."

"Yes, but—"

"You got busted?"

"Yes, and my mom refused to get me out, refused to

take me for counseling, so I had to do some time." Her juvenile record was sealed but Jack seemed thorough enough to find a way to get at it.

"Wait a minute. You numbered your stepfathers? No wonder you acted out."

"I'm on number seven now. They live in Miami. Been together about five years, so this one might actually stick." She laughed. "Besides, I'd like to believe that even *my* mother can find the real thing and hang on to it."

He chuckled along with her. "My parents divorced when I was in my teens. It was ugly. Neither of them have ever found the real thing."

"Maybe they had it and lost it?"

He shrugged. "What's worse? Never finding it or having it and letting it slip away?"

"The trick would be to find it, then to accept it as the real thing and hang on for dear life."

"Beautiful and smart."

Her chance to lead the conversation back to her days with Johnny DeLongo's gang faded, overtaken by the philosophy of love and loss. To lighten the mood, she changed topics.

"I've never seen such an expansive backyard."

He sipped from his water bottle. "The estate's too big now that Lindsay's moving out." One side of his mouth curled up. "A single-level will be easier for Rory in a few years."

More evidence of his innate kindness. Her heart warmed that he'd consider Rory's needs as time took its toll. "That's thoughtful."

"No, just practical. I hope you can meet Lindsay, but tomorrow's crazy. Maybe you'll cross paths in the kitchen for morning coffee."

"She's important to you."

His gaze softened. "I can't imagine not having her in my life. She looked up to me and filled the house with girly-girl stuff." His voice turned fond. "I'd find her stash of lipstick in my sock drawer when Rory said she was too young to wear it, and her room was plastered with posters of teenage heartthrobs."

She laughed. "Typical stuff." He'd opened his home and his heart to a young girl who'd been through a traumatic time. She did the math. When Lindsay moved in at eleven, Mac had been sixteen. Three years after his parents' divorce he'd brought in a child who'd taken on the role of kid sister.

"It was good to see her come around," he explained. "After the accident she needed months of physical therapy and counseling." He lowered his voice. "She was caught in the wreckage while her parents were dying in the front seat. She kept talking so her mother would stay with her. But her mother died anyway and Lindsay didn't speak again for a year."

Morgan blinked back tears. He was such a good, deeply caring man, she was afraid she could fall hard. She stood quickly, too aware, too edgy, too frightened of her own feelings to sit still. "I hope I can meet her." She muttered the platitude, afraid this man could take hold of her heart.

"You remind me of her," he said as he stood. "I saw it when you walked into the office and joined Jack and me. Most women would have stayed clear, but you decided I needed your help and you gave it, in spite of Jack's glare." He took her into his arms. "Lindsay's like that. Brave and fiercely protective when she needs to be."

"Oh." She had no response to such a compliment. She'd

barged in, been too impulsive, maybe even nosy! And here he was, calling her brave and fiercely protective.

It was too easy to flow into his embrace, like water into a quiet eddy. Held this way, she gave in to her need to caress and kiss, and mostly, to be held by this very real man with a heart that ran true and strong.

Whatever fantasies she'd harbored of Kingston McRae paled in the face of the real Mac.

She smoothed his broad chest, caught sight of her unvarnished, short fingernails and pulled her hand back. BB was much better at all the girly grooming. But inch-long nail tips weren't Morgan's style so she sucked it up and slipped her hand into his. His mouth went to her neck and he nibbled and kissed his way to her ear. She sighed and pressed her hips to his in invitation. "Let's go to bed. I need you."

"Music to my ears." His cock rose hard and ready as he rubbed lightly against her. "I can't keep my hands off you."

"I'm glad to hear you say that." More time with him was all she craved. "After we were interrupted, I thought I should leave." She laughed. "I guess Jack calling BB and getting us more time backfired on him. He wants me out of your life."

"Jack's at the office with his team working on the photographs and Rory's already gone." He led her through the slider to the den. "We have the rest of the afternoon. Or at least until Jack needs me again."

"Photographs?" She stalled and tugged him to a stop.

"Just pictures of me arriving at the airport on my jet."

"So that was the first security breach? You don't fly commercial." She'd never seen any airport photos of him.

"Someone knew when your jet would arrive and what hangar you use?"

"The fact that the package was delivered to the owner of a business I mentor is a message. They want me to know that I have no privacy—that they know everything I do, everywhere I go."

"No wonder Jack's so jumpy about me. It could be anyone, anywhere."

He shook his head. "This is someone who's peripherally connected to the household. Or used to be. I'm not worried about myself. Once Lindsay's away from here, she'll be safe. The wedding has to go off without a hitch."

7

"LINDSAY HAS NO IDEA what's going on?" Morgan asked Mac as they stood in the den.

"No, and we're not telling her. She's not to have one iota of concern on her wedding day."

Morgan warmed again at his kindness. But that wasn't top on her mind at the moment. It was sex. With him.

"Enough about that," he said as he tucked a strand of hair behind her ear, pulling her softness against his hard body.

"We have all the time we need." His hands cupped her head and he tilted her face to the right, then the left, but still, he didn't kiss her. "You're lovely. Your skin is perfection itself."

Perfection. "That's a nice thing to say." Heat rose in her cheeks.

His nose trailed close to her cheek, down her neck to her shoulder. "Your scent. Your skin. Your shorts."

"My shorts?" Ludicrous. She glanced up to see if he was joking.

"But only because they're at the top of your incredible legs." He kissed her cheek, slid his mouth to her neck.

Oh, yes!

She leaned into the warmth, needing more. She closed her eyes and shifted her weight closer. Her chest to his, her hands on his back. His fingers tightened on her arms in an urgency she felt to her toes.

Finally his mouth took hers in a light caress. Shivers ran the length of her as she responded to his delicate exploration.

She played his tongue with tentative strokes, her hands seeking. He could take her anywhere, any way he wanted. She moaned in submission.

He swept her into his arms and gathered her tight. The breath left her lungs, the strength left her limbs. Desire remained. A tide of desire that made her feel urgent, hungry and needful. She held his head and searched his lips with hers, imprinting the taste of him. When his tongue invaded her in insistent demand, she gave way. Let him have what he wanted. And what she needed.

He tasted of heat and want, of man and need, of sex and rapacious desire. His lips firmed and coaxed. She pressed up into him so her fingers could curl into his shirt and hold tight. Pulling him down to her, she took his mouth with her tongue and died with the wanting.

She rocked her hips against his and lost all trace of thought. His hands slid to her butt, cupped the fleshy mounds and lifted her hips deeper into his erection.

The groan low in his throat echoed her own, and he deepened the kiss.

He tangled her hair in his hands as he held her still to plunder her mouth. She tore at his zipper and tugged his slacks down. His mouth still on hers, he pulled her shorts off and shoved aside the thin strip of her thong. She groaned in pleasure when he plunged his finger into her.

"Mac." She sounded breathless. "More." He slid a

second finger inside and turned them to tease the nerve endings. She rocked again and bit her lower lip as her softest flesh eased to accommodate his probing. Her knees gave way and he shifted her so she could brace herself on the arms of the leather lounger.

"Like this?" But he was already there, at her entrance. She heard a packet open, the slick sound of latex, and he spread her feet wider.

He penetrated slowly, her channel adjusting to his fullness. When his fingers found her clit, need rose and she lost herself to him.

Each press and retreat came faster, harder, while he worked her into a frenzy. With an urgent cry he crashed against her and his body's powerful pulsation tipped her over the edge.

MORGAN ROLLED TO HER back, then propped herself up on one elbow to see if Mac had woken yet. His expression was calm, youthful, and she caught a glimpse of the boy he once was in the softened corners of his mouth and sweep of lashes beneath his closed eyes. His breath came deep and even as slumber still held him. Good.

She wasn't sure if she could manage another round. The spirit was willing but her flesh sore, and her heart was definitely in danger. She'd had the most incredible night of her life, with the most interesting man she'd ever met. Ever wanted.

But all good things, especially things that could never last anyway, had to end. She sucked up her disappointment, counted her blessings and slipped from the bed.

She ignored the twinges that came from a night of stupendous sex and got dressed quickly in the master suite bathroom. On a stack of fresh towels, she found the toothbrush and toothpaste Mac had provided. She brushed and rinsed quickly, sorry the mint flavor washed away the taste of him.

She pulled on her shorts and snapped the tab closed, then slipped back out of the bathroom and ran on tiptoe with her boots in her arms past a sleeping Mac.

She felt like a thief.

Which was wrong, because if anyone had stolen anything it was Mac. She was leaving behind a piece of her heart. She just hoped it wasn't a big piece, but if it was, she'd have to deal with the loss later.

Every word, chuckle and teasing moment between them had chipped away at her. Around midnight, they agreed the food they'd ordered in hadn't held up to the rigorous activity, so they'd crept downstairs to raid the kitchen. They'd returned to bed with meaty sandwiches and a bottle of beer each. Imported, of course.

They'd talked, confessed, exaggerated and laughed about all of it. He'd shared the details of his frustration with the medical teams he'd brought in for Lindsay. At only sixteen, he'd developed the dogged determination and team-building skills he relied on today.

She'd shared snippets of her life with a man-hunting mother. When he'd looked concerned, she'd assured him that she'd developed self-confidence and an independent streak, not to mention her in-your-face attitude.

But conversation had stalled and sex had taken over again and again. They'd been insatiable. One night was all she'd have of him, so she'd made the most of it.

She had to return to reality and her responsibilities. Talking about her past had reinforced the differences between Mac's life and hers. She was no Cinderella to be rescued by a man, not now, not ever.

At the front door Morgan slipped into her socks and

boots. She checked for the gate button and pressed it in case the mechanism by the gate was locked overnight.

The Morgan was still secure behind Bessie. She released the car and took off before she lost all sense and returned to Mac's bed.

She turned right at the end of the drive and managed to control the urge to look back until she was at a stop sign at the first intersection.

There, she put her head down on Bessie's steering wheel and drew in several deep breaths. She'd spent the night with Kingston McRae. Scratch that. He wasn't Kingston any longer. He was Mac.

She had yet to assess the damages. The piece of her heart she'd left behind was his. She would learn to live without it.

The roar of a motorcycle brought her attention back to the road. She glanced into her side mirror.

A big black bike moved up beside her, the rider half-naked. His head was encased in a midnight-black helmet, visor down. But there was no mistaking the broad chest and hard muscular arms.

Mac!

Her heart jumped into her throat as the bike came up beside her. He motioned her to lower her window.

He raised his visor and glared at her.

"What's wrong?" she asked as he pulled off his helmet. His hair still looked mussed from sleep.

"You took off!"

"I told you I had to leave first thing." She kept her voice huffy as if she didn't have time to speak with him... or the need to. But she drank him in one last time.

"Leaving is one thing, but sneaking out without a word is another. I don't have your phone number!"

Her belly dropped. Her throat closed around a gulp. "You want my number?"

A slow, lazy grin settled on his mouth. "I want your number. But I'd much rather you give it to me than make me ask Jack to get it. I need to know *you* want me to have it, Morgan."

WHEN MAC HAD HEARD the unmistakable sound of Bessie's rock and roll down the drive, he'd leaped out of bed and pressed his face to the window. All he'd seen was the back end of the creaking tow truck. Morgan had slipped out of his bed, and his life, without waking him, without so much as a goodbye.

He'd pulled on last night's slacks without underwear, socks, or a shirt. No shoes, either. Now he balanced the heavy bike on his toes, while he kept his feet away from the heat of the engine.

"Of course I want your number," he snapped. He reached into the cab of the truck and slid his fingertips down her cheek. "Spend today with me. Come to the wedding with me." The invitation came out of his mouth before he could stop it. But the moment it was there, in the air, it felt right. Everything about her felt right.

She flinched at the invitation, as if he'd said something to wound her.

"What's wrong?" he asked.

She shifted her slim shoulders and her gaze softened. "Mac. What we had, I'll never forget, but I like you more than is good for me." She laughed. "And don't you have enough on your plate without me getting clingy and needy?"

"You? Clingy? I doubt it." Had she just flexed her thighs in memory? The idea made him hotter than hot, and the burn through him had nothing to do with the engine between his knees.

"Here's the thing," he began again, "I like you, too. We make sparks when we touch and I want to explore where this could go." Bessie's diesel clicked and rumbled and then it hit him. "Why should we forget about each other just because you drive Bessie and I...don't."

She assessed him, clearly waiting for her bullshit meter to kick in. She opened her mouth, her eyes mutinous, so he spoke before she could refuse him. "It's Lindsay's wedding day, Morgan. I'm dateless. Take pity." He put on his best, most reasonable expression.

Her face crumpled as she burst into laughter. "You're such a fraud, Mac. You've never gone to any social event without a date."

"This is a family affair, not a social event." But her point had hit home. If he took her as his date, there could be speculation about who she was. She'd be a tabloid target. "If you drove the wedding party in the Morgan, no one would know who you are. What could one weekend hurt? If you never want to see me again after tonight, I promise I'll understand. This is a gift we can give ourselves. A slice out of our normal lives."

Her gaze slid from his head, lingered on his chest, then settled on his feet. A peeled apple under her gaze, he felt stripped of all that covered his flesh.

"Won't you burn your feet?" Her tone was husky.

He wanted her so much he could taste her.

"Not if I get home right away, but there's no time to waste." The neighborhood was waking up as they spoke. Cars pulled through the intersection, drivers curiously checking out the half-naked biker and the tow truck.

She noticed the gawkers. "I'll follow you."

Back at the house, the wedding dress designer had

already arrived. Bessie rumbled in behind him and Morgan parked beside the garage.

The designer and her assistant gave him a nod and slanted Morgan a curious glance when she climbed out of her truck. Morgan ignored the stares. The assistant carried a long garment bag held high in her arms while the designer lugged heavy satchels. The bridal gown and supplies. That meant the hustle and bustle of the day had begun.

"No back to bed for us," Morgan grumbled when she reached his side.

"We'll have tonight," he said, but she had already walked over to check out the Morgan's interior. She gave a low appreciative whistle. "You'll take Lindsay, Rory and me to the church, then drive the bride and groom to the reception, then on to the marina afterward so they can board the yacht for their honeymoon."

"You're serious? You'll let me drive this baby?" Her eyes shimmered. "You'd trust me with—"

"Why not? You've probably driven more vehicles than I have."

She pursed her lips. "Probably."

"This makes perfect sense." He'd hoped to be the first to street drive the Morgan, but it was a small sacrifice to have her with him for another day. "Lindsay thinks use of *The Glass Slipper* for their honeymoon is my wedding gift, so I need you to back me up when you meet her."

"*The Glass Slipper* is your yacht?" She rolled her eyes.

At his nod, she counted off on her fingers. "The church, the reception, then the marina and back here."

"Round trip about twenty miles or so. But you've got to vouch for me when I present her with the car. Just help me keep her moving. We can't give her time to think.

She's independent to a fault. Once she sits inside this baby, she'll accept that it's a done deal." There were a couple years when she first came to live with her grand-dad when every move had to be approved by a doctor or therapist. Lindsay had learned early to be a fighter.

"No problem," Morgan said. "I've had a lot of experi-ence with brides. I'll get her into the car." She smoothed her shorts and tugged at the bottom of her T-shirt. "But what will I wear?"

"I'll get Rory on it."

She was such a study in beauty. Perfect brows, lus-cious lips and a lovely jaw. Her ears were gracefully carved, he recalled, with delicious lobes. He tugged her into his arms and planted a light kiss on her lips. She responded immediately and rose to her toes, pressing close. Her neck smelled womanly and warm and made him crazy.

She made him crazy. Her tongue slipped shyly into his mouth, as if they hadn't spent the night locked together, as if this was their first tasting. She rocked him to his core.

Jack thought he was certifiable to let a strange woman into his life right now. Under the circumstances he should probably agree, but he wanted Morgan Swann again. Right now, if she'd have him. The soft moan from deep in her throat gave him the answer he craved.

He tore his mouth away from hers before he took her hard and fast the way he had in the den. "We'll find you clothes to wear." He barely got the words out. "Then later, I'll take them off you."

Rory appeared in the open front door. "There you are." He cleared his throat and gave a Mac a pointed glance. "No time to dress?"

"Change in plans, Rory. We need a black suit for Morgan. She's driving today."

"I have just the thing," Rory said without batting an eye. "When I broke my foot two years ago, we had that young fellow drive while I recuperated. He wasn't much taller than Miss Swann."

"Perfect," she said, her eyes lighting up. "And it's Morgan."

Mac chuckled. "I can't tell if it's driving the Morgan that's got you so happy or spending more time with me."

"My mother taught me to keep a man guessing."

Rory grinned at her as he walked to the dress designer's car. He pulled out a couple of cases. "I'm sure the designer will lend her assistant for a nip and tuck for Morgan." The gleam in his eye said he'd sized up the situation to a tee.

Sometimes Rory was a pain in the neck.

MAC HAD MORGAN JUST where he wanted her, getting pinned and basted into the spare chauffeur's uniform. The assistant stitched fresh seams into the jacket. When she knelt to check the hem of the pants, she clucked at Morgan's work boots. "You're kidding, right? These are, um…"

Morgan sighed. She didn't have suitable shoes at home, either. "What size does the bride wear?"

"She's close enough to your size," the assistant replied. "A pair of hers might work." She looked frazzled by the delay.

"I'll see what I can do." Morgan headed out and found Rory downstairs, accepting a flower delivery. He directed her to Lindsay's room in their personal quarters.

She tapped lightly and entered at Lindsay's surprised

hello. She was a soft blonde with a glowing beauty. Her dress was unwrapped and ready and her face shone with joy. She stepped toward Morgan with a breathtaking smile. "Hi! You must be Morgan. Granddad told me you're driving us to the church."

Her eyes said Rory had told her much more, but Mac appeared right behind Morgan, putting an end to any questions Lindsay might have asked.

Mac took charge of the introductions. One glance at Morgan's socks and he said, "Linds, do you have a pair of black loafers Morgan can borrow?"

"I'm a six and a half, but sometimes—"

"I'm a seven," Lindsay said and hurried to her closet. She knelt awkwardly on the floor, waving away Mac's offer to assist. "Voilà!" She turned with a broad smile and held up a pair of heavy black loafers. "Will these be okay? They'll add an inch because the soles are thick."

Morgan slipped her feet into the shoes. "They'll do. My socks take up a lot of room."

"Are the woolly socks okay?" Mac asked with a smirk. The veiled reference to how much he liked her socks shot an arrow of desire through her. The man was incorrigible.

Lindsay and Morgan shared a look, rolled their eyes and made shooing motions with their hands. Mac retreated with a wide grin.

"So, you're a new friend of Mac's?" Lindsay asked.

"I'm just your driver," Morgan assured her. "I don't expect to see today." Lindsay's honeymoon would likely last longer than her Mac-induced fever.

Lindsay sized her up with frank assessment and her eyes turned shrewd. "That's too bad, because he loosens up when he talks about you. That's unusual."

"Oh." She couldn't keep the surprise from her voice

and Lindsay winked. In that moment she looked a lot like her grandfather.

"I hope you're here when I get back from my honeymoon, Morgan." The dress designer clicked her tongue and Lindsay took the hint.

"That's nice of you to say," Morgan told her, then escaped.

Once the pants were hemmed, Morgan slipped out of the house in her uniform to check out the car. The Morgan was a spectacular machine.

In a deep, British-racing-car green, it looked like something out of a thirties movie. Round headlamps and sweeping fenders narrowed to actual running boards, giving the car a distinctive look. A deep, emerald-green convertible top finished the package. The car was a roaring beauty.

She bent down beside the driver's door and took a long look inside. When she'd been working with the Morgan before, it had been all business.

This gawking was pure appreciation.

MAC LEFT LINDSAY AND Morgan. Seeing them together, so easily in tune, brought a smile to his lips.

His cell vibrated in his pocket. It was Jack. "What have you got?"

"Our IT guys say the cracker was bouncing all over the Net. He edited all the logs of the ISPs he used. No way to say when we'll track him."

"Cracker?"

"Criminal hacker. This bastard knows what he's doing."

"If he's this skilled, then it's likely to be a crime ring—which means it's not personal." Relief seeped through his bones. He could go into the office, get back to his mentorship program. Have his private life stay that way.

"Not so fast. The airport photos and the security monitors make this about you specifically. This cracker is a weapon aimed directly at you."

"So stop him."

"You ready to let me bring in some men for the wedding?"

He closed his eyes and imagined Lindsay and Rory, dressed and excited. With Morgan disguised as a chauffeur, no one would know her connection to him. "The wedding guest list is fewer than fifty people. An intimate party of friends and family. I won't have a date, so this is not a photo op. There will be no media coverage. Security personnel will create a stir we may not be able to contain. I won't have them here." He disconnected because Lindsay stepped out onto the driveway, all grown up and ready to be a wife.

Mac's eyes stung at the sight. Rory proffered his arm and escorted her to the car, where Morgan held the door open.

"She's so lovely." Morgan sighed as Mac went to join her. "As many times as my mother's been married, I love seeing a bride."

While pretty, Lindsay wouldn't turn heads in a crowd, but she had a smile that drew a person in and warmed them through. Her smile was directed full on at Morgan and Mac, and her eyes gleamed with joy.

Mac didn't want to crush the dress, but Lindsay would have none of his standoffishness. She clasped him to her and blinked up into his face. "This is it, Mac. Do I look okay?"

"You are perfection, pure perfection. I hope Greg understands how lucky he is."

Rory said a quiet, "Hear, hear."

"He does," she promised.

"I want to give you your wedding gift, Linds."

"No! Mac, just no. There's nothing you could give me that you haven't already." She squeezed her grandfather's hand. "A home, a life."

His heart swelled as he opened one arm to encompass the car. "She's yours. Yours and Greg's, Linds. Enjoy her."

A full five minutes of arguments and soft-voiced threats followed, but in the end when Morgan pointed out they'd be late for the church, she gave in.

Lindsay settled in the Morgan's rear seat. She must be tired, but the glow on her face was pure joy.

Morgan helped gather the skirt of her gown for her, then waited while Mac settled into the front passenger seat. Rory sat behind Morgan and held his granddaughter's hand.

"I've never seen a more lovely bride," Morgan said. "It's an honor to drive you."

"I'm so nervous of stumbling. I hope I can manage all right in these shoes."

"Just look at the groom's face," Morgan suggested. "And you'll glide up the aisle."

Lindsay's face broke into a happy grin. "You're right! I feel better. Thank you, Morgan, you're very sweet."

"I've got lots of experience with weddings." Morgan winked at Mac and shared a heated look that promised heaven later.

"So how did you two meet, Morgan?" Lindsay asked. "Mac didn't say. Apparently, he's kept a lot of secrets lately." She leaned forward and flicked Mac's ear.

"Ow! Is this how you treat the men in your life?"

"Only the ones who are more trouble than they're worth," she teased him while Morgan started the car.

"It's a good thing I only ended up with one sister," he shot back. "I couldn't put up with another one like you."

In her excitement, she didn't notice that neither he nor Morgan had answered her question on how they'd met.

THREE HOURS LATER, Morgan settled into a chair in the outer hallway at the reception. She was the only uniformed driver, so she wasn't sure if she should be here, but Mac had insisted. He'd visited her a couple times, brought out a plate of finger foods and a bottle of imported water and even stolen a kiss.

Thankfully, her secret crush had been destroyed for what it was, a childish fairy-tale dream. Unfortunately, it had been replaced by a woman's infatuation. She was infatuated with a caring, intelligent, sexy man who liked her. She understood what she was dealing with and she'd be smart to get away as soon as she could.

Morgan could never compete with women who were on a first-name basis with their haute couture designers and Hollywood hair stylists. Hell, she didn't take spin classes or yoga or whatever was in with the rich and famous today.

She looked at her hands. She should have those sexy French nails made of gel or silk or acrylic instead of her work-length, sturdy fingernails. She buffed them once in a blue moon, mostly because BB dragged her over for a makeup session.

The thrill of driving the Morgan had reminded her of some of the other high-powered exotic cars she'd driven. This time it was refreshing to have the owner's permission. The wry thought reminded her of the differences in her life and Mac's. He'd gone joyriding in his dad's car while she'd ripped off vehicles and delivered them to chop shops.

He lived in the stratosphere of society, while she was grounded in the reality of a downtown neighborhood that had seen better days.

Yes, time would deal with their mutual infatuation and neither she nor Mac would be hurt when it was over.

Yeah, right.

8

MAC WATCHED LINDSAY as she enjoyed the best day of her life. In a waltz with her new husband, she glowed with love and pride. Greg was a lucky man and showed that he knew it with attentive glances and loving touches. Rory blinked away a sheen of happy tears every few minutes. He tapped the groom's shoulder to cut in and swept Lindsay into his arms.

"You look happier than I've seen you in ages," Lindsay commented.

"You haven't seen me in months. I was in Africa, remember?"

"Before you left you were on edge. I don't see that now. Is it such a relief to be rid of me?" She was teasing him, the way she always did when she wanted information out of him. If she turned the issue on herself, he'd rush to tell her about everything else in his life.

This was her way of asking about Morgan. Unfortunately he didn't have any answers for her. He kissed the tip of her nose. "If you want the unvarnished truth, I'm jealous."

She tilted her head. "Of what?"

"What you and Greg have." He turned the tables

and asked his own questions. "How did you get here? What path did you both follow to end up choosing each other?"

She blew out a breath and closed her eyes for a long moment. When she opened them again, they were moist. "I never expected to find a man like Greg. He's athletic, and so competitive I didn't think he'd look at a woman like me. I can't keep up with him physically and I—"

He dipped her to cut her off. "Shush. Not all men want physical perfection, Linds. Smart men look for more than that. And a smart man recognizes the right woman as soon as she shows up."

She chuckled. "Greg says he knew right away."

"See? He's a smart man." The man in question tapped his shoulder, wanting his bride back.

Mac handed her over, and let her go at the same time. She wasn't a frightened eleven-year-old girl anymore. She didn't need his home or his support—hadn't for a couple of years now. She could stand on her own physically and emotionally.

With her new husband at her side, Lindsay could take on the world and win. She'd changed into a powerhouse of a woman right under his nose. She had strength, confidence, the ability to think quickly and turn a blind eye to obstacles. He recognized the same qualities in Morgan.

Morgan.

She waited in the hall, dressed in a borrowed suit and shoes, looking like a million bucks. He grinned and wondered what she'd say if he told her how sexy she looked in a black fitted jacket, her wavy hair contained in a tight bun.

He wanted her here, dancing with him. He wanted to show her off, plain and simple.

But tonight wasn't the night. He couldn't bring attention to her yet. Before he could bring Morgan out from behind closed doors, he had to let Jack get to the bottom of this stalker business.

He couldn't recall the last time a woman of his choosing had been on his arm in public. A sad state of affairs.

Morgan was cool. Interesting. Fun. And he liked her.

He'd enjoy her company while he had the chance. Soon enough he'd settle back into a work routine. Jack would find the stalker and put an end to that nuisance. With a little luck, Mac would find the full-out commitment he witnessed between Lindsay and Greg.

He wanted what they had. It might be the wedding atmosphere, the best wishes flying high, the hopeful future they shared, but hell, he was thirty-four and it was past time to settle into a permanent relationship.

Once this stalker threat was neutralized, he'd work on finding the real thing. *If he hadn't already.* An image of Morgan came to mind and suddenly the few minutes of conversation they'd had weren't enough.

All he wanted was to get out of the party atmosphere and take her somewhere quiet. Acquaintances hailed him. He nodded back, firmed his lips as if he had somewhere important to be. Which was true. At this moment there was no more important place to be than with Morgan. He kept his expression focused and hoped no one would expect him to stop or chat.

Tables were being cleared while the quartet Rory had hired moved from the waltz to a faster number. People headed for the dance floor, blocking his efforts to move toward the exit. He aimed for the outer wall to skirt the crowd.

A server, loaded down with a full tray of dirty dishes, suddenly swung in front of him. He sidestepped to make his way around. At the near collision, the man glanced his way. "Sorry!"

"No problem," Mac responded.

"Hey, you're—"

"No, I just look like him," he said and moved on. He couldn't wait to see Morgan, all lush and pretty, her green eyes full of the joy of the day. He'd wanted to hold her hand on the way here, but she'd shifted gears constantly.

Lindsay liked her. In spite of the rush this morning, Lindsay had dropped what she had to do to find a pair of shoes for Morgan. A roll of the eyes, the kind of silent communication women were so good at, and he'd been banished.

He pulled open the door to the hall and stepped out, leaving the party sounds behind. Blessed quiet.

SHE KEPT TO HER PLAN of being seen but not noticed. Not that it mattered. Mac had barely glanced her way. He was clearly distracted. Business concerns most likely. He was a dedicated man when it came to those businesses he helped. Why he wasted his time was beyond her. She'd never grasped the concept of anonymous philanthropy. Why wouldn't he want to be lauded for helping the poor?

She chatted with another guest, while Mac made for the exit to the hall. A near collision with a server proved his distraction. Normally, Mac moved with the grace of a dancer.

"It's odd that a chauffeur drove to the wedding," she said to the woman seated next to her. "It's such a small affair. One would assume Mac would drive Lindsay to the ceremony."

"You'd think, except the chauffeur is a lovely young woman—Mac's slipped out to see her a couple of times. I saw him with her when I went to the ladies' room."

The rest of the babble floated above her while cold rage coursed through her veins, numbing her fingers. The wine sloshed in her glass, dribbling down the outside of the flute.

No wonder he hadn't bothered inviting a date. He was hiding one. Typical Mac. Public dates were for photo ops, and since this was such a nothing event, he hadn't bothered inviting anyone with whom he wanted to be seen.

She set down her wine flute, and with an apologetic smile to her table mate, set out after Mac.

What she saw when she cracked open the door to the hall put her on edge. Mac was staring at the chauffeur as if he wanted to devour her. A redhead!

Once, she'd been the object of that desire. Mac had looked at *her* that way. She wanted that again.

Would have it again.

She ground her teeth to keep from flinging the door open. The prize was much bigger than a moment's wounded pride, and tipping her hand went against all her plans.

Instead of storming the hallway, she wedged the very pointed toe of her stiletto between the door and the frame so she could watch him and his whore. This time, she didn't bother trying to still the tremors in her hands.

Mac took in the sight of Morgan, all prim in her high-necked uniform. Her subdued hair looked more red than it had outside. A visceral punch of desire hit low and fast.

She lifted her gaze at his soft greeting, her eyes alight.

She liked him. She was happy to see him. She wanted him.

All those messages rolled down the sixty-foot hall and barreled into his chest.

"I'm glad you stayed and didn't go out to the car." If anyone else saw her expression, they'd guess immediately she was more than a chauffeur. God, he wanted her, here, now.

Right now.

She stood, eagerly holding his gaze. "Is that what real chauffeurs do?" she asked while her eyes begged for his touch.

To a man used to women who wanted everything but him, she was beyond believable.

Infinitely desirable.

He took her hand and pulled her into the dark coat check booth. The swinging door swished closed while he held her still for a deep kiss. His tongue searched hers, his hips strained close, while she cupped his ass and held him tight. Soft! Her lips were soft and warm, her center softer still as he pressed his hard length against her. If she'd worn a skirt he'd be inside her already. As it was, he tugged at the waistband of her slacks.

"Mac, we can't—not here." Hope glazed her voice in sexual need and he wanted to howl.

"Yes, we can." He eased her slacks halfway down her hips so his hand could fit between her thighs. She was already wet.

"Yes! Crazy, but yes." Her breathy whisper drove him higher.

But his need came wrapped in vulnerability and startled him. He didn't like it, but there wasn't a damned thing he could do about it, especially not with his arms full of this particular willing woman.

He walked her backward toward the wall. Her head barely cleared the rod, setting the empty hangers into a jangling racket. A shiver slid down his neck as he listened for any sound from the hallway. A feeling of being watched made him stop and raise his head to listen.

But Morgan pulled him back to her with another searing kiss. She slid her palms to his lapels and hung on, while she settled against the back wall of the booth. Her jacket fell off and he made short work of the buttons on her crisp white shirt. Her glorious breasts spilled into his hands when he lowered the cups of her bra. He tasted one, then the other, sucking them deeply. She sighed and held his head in place. *As if he needed help.*

She slipped her fingers into his open zipper and squeezed his hottest flesh. When she palmed his sac, his balls tightened in hot need.

He dived into her mouth time and again, kissing her whenever she went to speak. Ready to break all control, he tilted his forehead to hers. "Let me, Morgan. Let me take you there."

Her answer was simple.

She widened her stance, allowing his hand enough room to fully cup her wet need. Her breath went as ragged as his, her hair mussed. Telltale marks on her creamy skin showed where he'd nipped her the night before.

He kissed each one while his finger entered her and pressed deep inside. "I'm sorry I left my mark."

He loved that with him she was soft and yielding, because he didn't want to be in this alone. Vulnerable was a bad place to be on your own. He needed to brand her, to make her his. His mouth on her neck had made her crazy last night, and did again now. She licked her palm to get it wet then reached for his cock again and stroked him faster and faster while she squirmed on the edge of climax.

"Please, Mac," she said on a shaky breath. He pushed deep into her.

She offered her lips and he took them again and again, unable to see anything but Morgan. She tasted of impatience and a need that matched his own.

She moaned as his thumb massaged her clit. Her head rolled back, exposing more of her creamy flesh. The feel of her wet and needy beneath his hand while she stroked him took him past control.

Doubly aroused, they stroked and rubbed and kissed each other into oblivion. When she came, he held her mouth with his, her sighs and moans for his ears alone. Her thighs convulsed around his hand as moisture coated her sensitive flesh.

A dark possession came over him as her scent rose and her fingers tightened, taking him beyond arousal and into release.

This time she was the one to receive his groans as she stroked and held him tight. He emptied into her hand, ready to fall at her feet.

"Stay with me, Morgan. For as long as you can." He pressed against her most sensitive flesh. "Please."

"Uh…" She sighed against his mouth, let him taste the desire on her tongue. "You cheat. I…" She sucked in a breath, suspended while he held her. He rubbed a finger against her hottest need while her shuddering release eased away. "You make me all kinds of stupid, Mac."

"Stupid. Yes, me, too."

He moved in for another kiss, but before he could get more than a taste of her, sounds from the hallway filtered through the closed door. He hated to stop but he had no choice. "Sorry, I have to make an appearance."

"We shouldn't have come in here," she admonished, but her eyes were full of mischief.

"Like hell. I needed this." Like a teenager, he wanted her to be as crazy for him as he was for her.

She stood on her tiptoes and whispered against his ear, "So did I."

A murmur of voices filtered into the coat check. Feet shuffled in the carpeted hallway and the sound pulled them apart. He would never forget the look in her eyes, the flush of loving that made her so beautiful she took his breath.

She worked her buttons back into place. Then tucked in her shirt. He got busy and tidied himself as best he could.

He tilted her chin up with a fingertip. "Tonight, Morgan. I promise we'll go slow and gentle." His voice came out a hoarse whisper.

Hers was throaty. "I loved this. Loved the fast and hard and quick and dirty. I've never done anything so wild."

He chuckled and wondered what the *World Courier* would make of the playboy who could truthfully say the same thing.

"Follow my lead." He smoothed his hair with one hand while he opened the door and joined the guests in the hall.

Morgan slipped out behind him, her lipstick smeared off and her lips puffy. He'd give anything to acknowledge her place with him here, among friends and family. She might be surprised at his turn of mind because Morgan didn't believe she belonged.

The server Mac had sidestepped earlier stood in a corner. He slipped something into his pocket while he looked from Mac to Morgan. Just before he headed back into the dining hall, he gave Mac a lascivious wink. Mac frowned and wanted to follow the guy, but Lindsay approached to tell him she and Greg were ready to leave.

Only a handful of guests planned to follow the happy couple to the marina to see them off. Rory and Mac caught a ride with one of Lindsay's cousins whom Mac had met many times. Settled in the backseat, he checked his voice mail and found several messages from Jack. He hated to be drawn back into the hustle of the wedding and this stalker business after being with Morgan.

He made polite excuses to the cousins and called Jack.

"Tell me you've found answers." He kept his voice low, but even with friends and family, he was wary of leaks from "informed sources."

"I've had a call from Captain Redding. He and his crew are on the dock. *The Glass Slipper*'s been impounded for unpaid slip fees."

"That's impossible." He fought to keep his voice down. "Slip fees are just rent. Of course they've been paid."

"People are walking away from debt, trying to sell boats or defaulting on their fees." Of course, being the ultimate toy, a boat was one of the first luxuries people tried to unload. Problem was, no one else was buying. "This is someone who knew we wanted to use *The Glass Slipper.* If they could hack into a car dealership's system, then the marina would be easy pickings." This should help narrow the field of suspects. He told Jack that the groom had kept a tight lid on their honeymoon plans.

Rory got the chat to flow while Mac sat in a stew of outrage. His stomach churned with a combination of helplessness and the need for revenge. When he found out who was doing this, he'd destroy him.

"OH, HONEY, I'M SORRY. I guess I've been so rattled with the wedding that I forgot the yacht's in for maintenance." Rory shook his head and looked confused and contrite at the admission.

Lindsay hugged him. "It's all right, Granddad, really. Greg and I will go to a hotel instead."

Greg had already herded the guests back to the parking lot. Thankfully, not many had come along.

Rory's skill at prevarication impressed the hell out of Mac. It was a great show, but when Lindsay looked concerned enough to want to put off her honeymoon, Mac leaned in to Rory. "Let's not overdo it."

Then he turned to Lindsay and winked. "We'll explain all this when you get back. Your granddad's as sharp as ever. I've got a situation, that's all. I'll call a friend to borrow another vessel. No problem. He owes me a favor."

After a long, steady stare into his eyes, and then into Rory's, Lindsay agreed to use his friend's yacht. "Morgan, please keep in touch." The women hugged and Lindsay whispered something Mac couldn't catch.

Morgan went pink and nodded. "If you think so," she said quietly.

THREE HOURS LATER, Morgan had given Mac the driver's seat and they were on their way back to the estate.

She clasped his hand in her lap, gave it a gentle squeeze. His driving style was lazier than hers. He got into fourth gear and kept it there for as long as possible.

She resisted the urge to tell him to downshift. "Still no idea who might want to mess with you this way?"

"No." He shrugged. "I've racked my brain, but this is so personal it's hard to figure. I keep going back to business connections and come up empty. This person has details of my life that only someone relatively close to me would have. But how could a friend or associate be this off the wall without me noticing?"

"They hid it well. Don't blame yourself for being a target." She gave in to her urge. "You could be in third gear here."

He grinned, then downshifted. "Yes, dear."

"See that you pay attention from now on," she teased. "A car like this likes to be driven." She hoped she sounded prim.

He laughed. "You're priceless."

She looked out the passenger window, absurdly pleased.

"I agree with Morgan," Rory said from the backseat. "If it's not personal, it must be business. Perhaps from years past."

Mac glanced in the rearview at Rory, then at her. "I retired quietly from aggressive business a couple of years ago. I still sit on a few boards. Do some charitable work. But these days I mentor neighborhood businesses. None of them would attack me this way."

"You retired quietly?" she asked. She hadn't read anything of the sort in the *Courier*. He'd been brilliant at keeping his real life out of the spotlight. The red-carpet beauties had been camouflage, nothing more. Which gave her pause.

Then cheered her up.

"Once I started to mentor entrepreneurs I enjoyed it so much, I kept with it."

"How do you find these people? If you pick and choose from a group of applicants you could make an enemy of someone you refused." She thought of a reality show where people were kicked out. But Mac would never behave so cavalierly with people's hopes and dreams.

"Businesses come to my attention in various ways. Sometimes it's an ad in a paper that catches my eye. If I like the concept, I'll watch how the business is run. If there's potential, I approach them on the *QT*. No one's yet broken their promise of silence."

"They wouldn't jeopardize more help and advice from you." She also understood he had to keep this quiet. "You'd be overrun if this got out."

"I keep my charitable foundation under wraps for the same reason. Unscrupulous people use fake charities to scam donations."

Rory joined in. "Mac has encouraged a lot of success through his mentoring program." There was a note of pride in his voice. "After a year or so, decent local jobs are created. The businesses that he takes an interest in thrive."

Mac shrugged. "It's fun. Gives me a charge to see it all work. It's satisfying to help build a business. I've made some interesting friends."

"I bet you have." He'd have met all kinds of people from all walks of life. His interest in her seemed more real. More honest.

He turned onto his street and swore. "What now?"

One of the security company cars blocked his gates. The driver climbed out and approached the car. "Mr. McRae, your power went off about fifteen minutes ago. Then your emergency backup lights came on. I've just checked the perimeter and the house is untouched. The office reports no intruders. Your cameras are fully functional. We can't see a reason for the loss of power, but—" He shrugged. "I thought I'd stick around anyway, just in case."

Rory grumbled darkly in the backseat and Morgan felt like doing the same.

"The emergency power won't operate the gates, but they'll open manually. That's how I got in to check the exterior of the house. There were no signs of a break-in attempt, but if you'd prefer, I can call the police."

"No need," Mac said. "We can check all the windows and doors from inside."

After he parked in front of the garage, Mac dropped his arm over her shoulders and tucked her close to his chest. His body warmed hers as she slipped her arm around his waist. "I've wanted to do this all day," he said in her ear.

"Why?"

"To show you off." He looked down at her, his eyes mysterious while his lips turned up at the corners. He was hard to read sometimes. The nuances of his expressions would take a while to learn, not that she would have that kind of time.

"Home again at last," Rory muttered behind them. "If this person set out to ruin my Lindsay's wedding, they failed. She was happy and glowing, just the way a bride should be."

"We covered things pretty well, Rory. It was quick of you to look so confused about *The Glass Slipper.*"

"I hope Lindsay's not worried about my mental faculties." Rory tapped his temple.

"I'd say by now Lindsay's not worried about much of anything." Mac kept his arm over her shoulder as they walked into the house through the garage entrance. It was dark in the foyer.

"The timer must have blown when the power went out," Rory said. He cursed a big ugly, then flipped a switch and the foyer flooded with light. He apologized to Morgan for his outburst. "I was in the Navy for a time," he said by way of explanation.

She chuckled. "No problem. I am the queen of blurting things I shouldn't."

Rory's shoulders sagged and he gave her an appreciative look. "A few years ago I would have kept a cool head with all that's been going on, but not now." Mac told her earlier that Rory felt bad for having allowed the phony security dude onto the estate.

"I didn't like walking into a dark house, either," Mac said, "not under these circumstances. We'll check that all the doors and windows are locked, then I'll walk the grounds and make sure the garden shed is secure. Morgan can head on upstairs." He gave her a kiss on the forehead. "I'll be up soon."

She didn't like the idea of Mac being outside in the darkness alone. "I'd like to walk with you," she said.

"I don't want you out there. Please head up to bed." His eyes said that was where he wanted her. Waiting for him in his bed. She could argue, but the security guard had said there was no sign of intruders on the grounds.

MAC WATCHED HER GO, then followed Rory into the kitchen. He found him checking the doors that led to the patio. "If this bastard is close enough to know we wanted the yacht today, then it stands to reason he also knows about the secret door in the shed."

"A very short list of people know about that." They might also know that it was the only egress that wasn't covered by cameras and motion detectors. The shed was a typical garden shed, except for a false back wall that

concealed a narrow door. The outside was well camou-
flaged with bushes.

"There's a good chance the stalker is not a he."

"Except the door hasn't been used to bring women
onto the estate since my father's adventures in the pool
house."

The last time the door had been used with any regularity was during Lindsay's teens, when she sneaked out
after being grounded.

"The women Jack's looking at don't have the expertise
to hack protected computer systems. That skill takes
dedication. Gretchen, Lila and Maria were dedicated to
beauty, style and their careers. There's no way they spent
years in front of a computer."

But a man who spent years on a computer would do
a lot for a beautiful woman. "Jack's got to look hard at
the men around those women." He hated to think that
any of the women were behind this, but at this point, he
couldn't ignore anyone.

After his call to Jack, he spent the night with Morgan,
lost in her. He loved the way she fit perfectly against him.
Her legs were long and strong and held him close while
he claimed her time and again.

They raided the kitchen around midnight, the way
they had the night before. Morgan perched on a stool
at the island counter, her taut sexy body covered by his
white formal shirt. The sleeves were rolled to her elbows
with precision folds that reminded him of her thick rolled
socks. He barely managed to keep his hands off her, but
hunger beat back his desire. Barely. The omelet in the
pan claimed his halfhearted attention.

Her voice came to him softly. "Have any of your girlfriends gone to the tabloids with juicy bits?"

He shook his head. "There weren't any juicy bits." He

glanced at her over his shoulder. She looked pensive, chin in hand, her hair mussed and sweeping her shoulders. But her eyes were wide with concern. It touched him in a way he would never have expected. She'd defended him, been fierce for him, and now she worried about him. At his comment, she rolled her eyes.

"Right, and those women didn't sit at this counter and watch you cook for them."

"That's right. They didn't." He faced her. "And I didn't."

She cocked her head. "So, their visits here weren't intimate?"

"I didn't say that. I just—" He wanted to get this right, get this perfect. "I didn't share myself in the same way I do with you."

Her expression was pleased and amused.

"And I didn't sleep with all of them, although I'm not sure why I'm telling you that." It was important for her to understand that he could be honest, too. "Except you should know I'm careful about women."

"Careful," she repeated. It wasn't a question, but a thoughtful statement. "I'm careful, too. I haven't had a lot of serious relationships. Maybe it's because my mom's had so many. I understand careful, Mac."

He lifted the cooked omelet onto one large plate, then set it down on the counter and slid a couple of forks across to her. As he rounded the counter to sit beside her, she jumped down off the stool. They collided softly, he with his hands up to steady her, she with her knee between his legs. She moved her leg, giving him a sexy rub with her thigh.

Witch. His libido woke, stretched and growled in his belly, so he grabbed her butt and held her tight against his growing erection.

She pretended not to notice. "Ketchup?" she asked.

He could get it for her, but he liked the idea of her making herself at home. "In the fridge."

When she put a blob on her side of the plate, he dipped a forkful of omelet into it. "Want your own?" she asked with a crook of her eyebrow.

"I'll just steal from yours."

She chuckled and turned the plate so the ketchup sat at twelve o'clock.

"It's amazing none of your exes have sold stories to the tabloids. Is it because you're such a decent man?"

"Just lucky, I guess." But he wondered how long his luck would hold.

9

Our favorite playboy Kingston McRae is slumming with the help! Caught in a tryst, McRae is seen here with his chauffeurette, looking well kissed.

MONDAY MORNING, MAC glared at the headlines in the *World Courier*. He was on the phone with his PR head, Cassie Ranger. "The photo came from a server with a camera phone at the wedding. Find out which of the jackals at the tabloid is after Morgan. I need to know everything they have on her."

"Yes, sir. I'll get back to you right away."

The next call was to Jack. "The *World Courier* has a front-page photo of Morgan and me looking—"

"I see it, I just pulled it up online. Wow. What were you thinking?"

"I wasn't." She'd been so hot for him, so completely giving, she blew his mind. And look what he'd done to her. Her privacy was gone, her life changed. "The headline spells it out."

He'd love to find that server just to wipe the lascivious smirk off his face.

The stunned silence from the other end emphasized

how stupidly he'd behaved. He never should have put Morgan into a position that could embarrass her. Jack found his voice. "I told you we needed a team at the wedding. At the least, I should have been there."

"My decision, my fault. Even you can't be in two places at once." He read further. "At least they've got her name wrong. They identified her as Morgan *Swain*. That'll give us time to bring her here, out of harm's way."

Silence. "You're sure you still want to be involved with her? It might be better to just let this die."

"How? Aside from my feelings for Morgan, I've put her in a rotten situation. I've just spoken to Cassie in PR. She's on the phone with her contacts at the *Courier*. They won't stop digging until they get more on Morgan, but it would help if we know what they know. Maybe we can prevent an all-out frenzy."

"Good. How's Morgan handling this?"

Surprised Jack would care, he admitted he hadn't spoken to her since yesterday. "I'll call when I have answers for her. I want to know who's on this story at the *Courier*."

Jack made a noise in his throat. "The woman drives a tow truck, Mac. She's got no experience with paparazzi."

"Is that a change of heart about her, Jack?"

"I'm still not sure she's the good woman you think she is, but she's a sitting duck with no idea who's coming for her. Her life could turn into a living hell." A thin note of sympathy leaked into Jack's voice. "She could still be on the make, though."

"Let's deal with what we know, not what you're making up in your suspicious mind." He hung up. Damn Jack for raising questions. It was his job, it was what Mac paid him good money to do. But it didn't sit well to have him question Morgan's integrity. It was in her eyes, those deep pools of soft green rimmed by sherry that sparked so brightly when she laughed. He'd also seen her honesty when she'd admitted to the joyriding. Helping yourself to someone else's vehicle was an odd thing for a teenage girl to do, but Morgan was not your typical female.

The image in the tabloid was clear enough to give his memory a hit. Her lips were puffy, her neck still pink from where he'd nipped her. He could taste her skin, conjure the softness of her breasts, the weighty feel of them in his hands. The way she'd climaxed on his hand had taken him into the stratosphere.

He had to convince her to stay with him. If no more photos surfaced, the story would die in a couple of days. Maybe there'd be an ugly divorce or custody battle with an A-list actor to take the heat off Morgan.

She'd left in the late afternoon on Sunday. He'd been on the phone with Jack when she'd bussed his cheek and walked out with a wave.

The breezy way she'd left had seemed fine at the time, but when he looked back on it, her smile was brittle and her eyes dark. It was clear she felt intimidated by their differences. He saw them as interesting quirks to be explored. He wanted to know what made her who she was, why she drove a tow truck, how she'd ended up with a job that seemed so out of the ordinary for a petite woman with a body that could stop traffic. They'd touched lightly on all these topics, but he wanted more.

"Mr. McRae, it's Cassie. They know her real name is Swann. They planted the wrong name as a red herring for the other papers. They've got her place of work and her home address. They know what school she dropped out of and are looking into a long absence from school when she was about fifteen."

"They planted a wrong name in the paper?"

"That gives them a jump on the competition for the next piece. They're going after her, sir. And they've got one of their most determined people on the story."

"Morgan's not a story. She's a friend. Can't you call in a favor to have them bury this?"

"I tried. They won't budge. I think this may be the end of feeding them what we want them to know. Hiding your charitable work and your mentoring will be impossible now."

"Do what you can, and thanks." He'd just put the receiver back on the cradle when it rang again. "Jack?"

"We've caught a whiff of something, Mac. Does the name Jonathan Lake ring any bells?"

"No. It could be a town or an actual lake."

"We're checking all the possibilities."

"Keep me informed. And Cassie tells me it's time to circle the wagons."

"Shall I go get Morgan, or will you?"

"I'll try. There's no telling how she'll react to this."

THE HEADLINES SCREAMED across the page but it was the picture that brought on the rage. Morgan Swain? That auburn-haired bitch from the wedding!

She was the one who'd driven the tow truck onto his estate. The truck that had been parked in front of his house for two nights in a row.

Five Aces Towing. That was the name on the door. Hacking into the dealership had been so easy. Who'd have thought it would backfire this way? What was Mac thinking, taking up with a woman like that?

It was bad enough to see her in a chauffeur's uniform,

but a tow truck was just too much. She shuddered at the idea of Mac's mouth on hers. His hands on her body. Jealousy and righteous rage twisted as images of Mac and this…this…slut twined together.

She'd wondered about that Mona woman. Thought that by delivering the airport photos to her, she'd have proof he was sleeping with her. But Mona had dropped the package off and left almost right away. Since then, she and her family had gone to a hotel. At least someone was taking things seriously.

The paper lay faceup on the hotel bed. She tilted her bottle of nail polish over the photo, let the crimson drops obliterate the bitch's face.

Morgan Swain had to be taken care of. Nothing drastic. Not yet. But this whore would be out of Mac's life or else.

First things first. She called Jonathan. "I want the addresses of the personnel who work at a trucking company called Five Aces Towing in Seattle. Do it now. I'm looking for the name Morgan Swain." She ran her fingertip through the crimson splotch over the whore's face.

MORGAN'S MONDAY MORNING started off just like any other. She woke on time, showered like usual, detangled her hair and caught it in a ponytail. She slapped her ball cap on her head, and for a change, slicked on lip gloss. She slid the gloss tube into the front pocket of her shorts and hit the back stairs of her apartment building at a dead run to get Bessie.

Twinges that reminded her of the great sex she'd had all weekend went ignored. She also ignored the sunny skies and the birds heralding the day. Mind deliberately blank, she headed for her usual coffee kiosk, where her favorite morning muffin awaited her.

The blankness lasted until she was in the lineup for the order window. With Bessie rumbling around her, she wondered what Mac had done on Sunday evening. Worked, probably. He'd said earlier that he had a lot of catching up to do.

All evening she'd been on edge, waiting for him to call, dreading it at the same time. But she couldn't stay with him another night. For one thing, she needed fresh clothes. For another, she hadn't wanted to talk about a future that couldn't happen.

It had been a fun fantasy, but she lived in the land of reality. Reality was Bessie, stinking of diesel, and BB chiding her about men. Reality was how she paid her bills.

And then there were the lies she'd told. Inadvertent as they were, she'd still lied. She hadn't confessed the whole truth about her days as a car thief, and when Jack finally dug out the story, Mac would look at her with different eyes. He'd see her for what she was: a phony.

Add that to the fact that she'd vowed never to need a man to rescue her: independence and freedom meant everything to her, and a relationship with Mac McRae was impossible.

A fantasy was best lived in the mind and had no place in her real life.

She inched Bessie to the window, where her regular barista smirked like a hooker with a secret. Bessie idled noisily while Morgan waited for her latte and muffin. When the barista snickered at her, she had to ask, "What's so funny?"

"I never see my regulars standing up," he said. "Until this." He pressed the front page of the *World Courier* to his window so she could get a good long look. "This is *you*, right?"

Her stomach slid to the floor as she took in the photo. Mac looked so handsome, so endearingly rumpled from loving her.

She squeezed her eyes shut and held her hand out for her latte and muffin. If the guy in front of her would just move his Lexus, she'd floor Bessie and get the hell out of here.

The tabloid had zoomed in on her and Mac looking like they'd just rolled out of bed. Heat rose at the memory of climaxing on his hand.

Surely Mac would be safe from this kind of spying at a family function? But it wasn't just family who'd been there. Anyone could have seen Mac take her into the coat check booth. Maybe one of the hired help needed a few bucks. Who didn't these days?

She offered the barista a five-dollar bill for the paper. He gladly handed it over. "Thanks!"

She drove out of the narrow lane, avoiding so much as a glance at the paper. For all of fifteen seconds.

Once she'd pulled into a parking spot, she pored over the article.

Her stomach roiled.

Her image was clear enough that the barista, a relative stranger, had recognized her. The name they got was only one letter wrong. But it was close enough. Her stomach constricted.

Mac mustn't know yet. They'd spent Sunday morning making love, raiding the kitchen, using the hot tub and playing video games. But by the afternoon, Jack had intruded with call after call about the investigation until she realized the truth.

The fantasy weekend was over and she'd be smart to put it into perspective and get back to reality-ville.

More weekends and lazy days spent in bed with Mac

would not happen. Maybe with some other woman, but not her. Maybe he'd find the perfect match Morgan could never be.

She considered calling him to explain that she hadn't arranged for the photo to be taken, but there wasn't any point. Jack had probably already accused her of orchestrating the photo, especially if he'd dug up her association with Johnny's gang.

Not that Mac would care that their tryst had been exposed. He was a single, heterosexual male. He'd probably get high-fived for boinking the help.

She folded the tabloid and put the front page facedown then drove on to work. Her last normal morning had only been a few days ago. Thursday, the day she and Joe had nabbed the Charger.

Before then she'd been edgy and, she hated to admit it, sex-starved. At least now she had the memory of Mac to fall back on when times got dark or lonely. For one shining weekend, she'd been his woman, cosseted and cared for. She'd played and made love with her fantasy man.

No one could take that away from her.

Still, it was time to forge ahead. There were recoveries to make, people to track and vehicles to tow. She looked forward to the surge of adrenaline that came with each adventure.

Seeing BB's car in her usual spot proved that in spite of the tabloid story, this Monday was like any other. She considered leaving the cringe-worthy newspaper behind, but BB would have an interesting take on it.

One look at her friend and the whole concept of a normal day went out the window. The unflappable BB was jumpy and nervous.

Morgan took a deep breath, held it and braced for

trouble. "What's up?" Maybe BB had already seen the tabloid.

"I screwed up this weekend," BB said. "Bad."

"Did your uncle find out we fudged on recovering Mac's Morgan?"

BB dismissed the question with a flick of her wrist. "Once I got the whole picture from Jack Carling and your Kingston McRae ponied up a deposit, it wasn't a problem." She leaned close in spite of the office being empty. "This is about Joe."

"Is that a blush I see?" BB blushing didn't happen often. "Wait a minute. You and Joe? You didn't!"

BB scrunched her face and nodded.

"You did!"

Her blush deepened.

"You two are so hot for each other, this place should spontaneously combust."

BB's whole demeanor had changed over the weekend. She glowed, looked lovely and lush and hmm...sated. Must be something in the air, because Morgan felt like she was looking in a mirror.

Still, something was *off* about BB. "Where are your eyelashes?" she asked. BB never forgot her full black set. "You look half-dressed."

"They came off."

"So, why didn't you stick 'em back on?"

BB went bright, fire-engine red.

"Where and how did they come off?" Suspicion rose. "Were you with Joe at the time, all hot and sweaty?"

"You could say that. One of them kind of tangled in his, um..." She stood abruptly and headed for the coffee station. As ample as her boobs were, her butt was just as lush. Encased in a spandex miniskirt, it barely moved.

BB was firm, even if she was a plus-size gal. "His, um…
oh, don't make me say this."

"In his chest hair?" Morgan held in bubbles of laughter, but it wasn't easy.

"Lower." BB's voice quivered and the coffee carafe
clattered back onto the warming plate. Her shoulders
jiggled. "Don't make me say it."

"His *pubes?*" Morgan blurted. She had to be wrong.
She shouldn't have said it. But when BB kept up the silent
giggles, Morgan blanched. "Your eyelash got tangled in
his pubes?" She hooted with laughter. At least she wasn't
alone in her insane behavior with men. Nothing she did
with Mac could top this, tabloid or no tabloid.

"You shush, it isn't funny." BB turned back to her
and rolled her bare-looking eyes. "Okay, it was a little
funny." A giddy light shone in her eyes and she bit her
lip. "After the first one came off, he asked for the other
one."

"And?"

BB tried and failed to deadpan her expression. "He
propped them—propped them!—on either side of his
penis. It looked like a nose. A very long, thick nose."
She collapsed against the filing cabinet and laughed. "A
face with droopy eyelids!"

Morgan was thunderstruck. BB was sleeping with a
nutbar. A sexy, appealing guy who also happened to have
a wild sense of fun.

She must be crazy about Joe, because she never, ever,
ever dated any of the crew.

"Oh. My. God. BB, you're in love!" It had been weeks
since BB had gone out clubbing. Three weeks to be exact,
ever since Joe had been hired.

She straightened. "No, I'm not! I'm not in love. Joe
and I are having a few laughs and some great sex." Her

face glowed as her mind seemed to focus on a memory. "Really, really great sex." She sobered. "But enough about me. What happened with Kingston McRae?"

"It was fabulous. Dreamy. I'll never forget it." Or him.

"But?"

"It's got to be over sometime. I have to be realistic."

BB nodded and indicated the decor in the old gas station. "You mean this wouldn't meet his standards?"

"Something like that."

"Did he figure out you have a crush on him?"

"No. But I let that go when I realized he's not the man the *World Courier* thinks he is." She shrugged. "I also didn't quite get around to telling him about my record. Why ruin the fantasy with the awful truth? We had a fabulous time. No regrets, no expectations. Seriously, the guy's so far out of my league." She crossed her arms to contain her confused emotions. "Every time I mentally prepared myself to leave Mac's estate, he'd look at me with this *I want you* expression and I'd cave in and stay." She sighed softly at the memory of his oak-colored gaze heating her up. "And that was *so* not good for me. I mean, I was flattered, but I have to get my priorities in order." She had to stop playing at being Cinderella.

BB looked ready to say more, but Morgan put up her hand to stop her. "If there were a chance for something more—" she held out her copy of the *World Courier* "—this would definitely put an end to whatever might have been."

BB read the headlines then gaped in shock at the photo of Morgan. "Oh, no! How?"

"I'm betting on a camera phone."

"Of course." She looked disgusted. "Those things

cause way more trouble than they're worth. What will you do?"

Morgan waved her hand in dismissal. "Get back to work." She shrugged. "Mac's the story, not me."

"I wouldn't be too sure about that."

"When I'm on the road, I'll move fast and keep moving. They'll pick on someone else soon." She tapped the photo and BB went back to scanning the paper for details.

"What does Mac say? Is he angry?"

"I haven't heard from him."

"It's creepy that whoever is stalking Mac may be looking at this picture of you right now," BB said. "If anyone comes asking questions about you, I'll call Jack Carling," BB said. "He'll want to know."

"It's okay to tell him." Not that she ever cared to see the guy again. "Remember, he's prematurely gray."

"I'll remember the silver fox."

Even if he was wrong about her, Morgan admired the man's forthright demeanor. "More like an Arctic wolf. Predatory and stone cold."

BB quirked her eyebrow. "I checked around and no one has any other recoveries aimed at McRae. It was the Morgan and the yacht. That's it."

"Maybe this is all some horrible mistake then." She picked up three work orders before BB could cross the floor and stop her.

"Morgan! I haven't sorted those yet."

"That's okay. If I see anything that looks the least bit hairy about any of these, I'll call for backup."

"Promise me."

"I promise. I need to keep busy."

BB made a doubtful noise and narrowed her gaze. "You can't bury your feelings for Mac under a ton of work." Her eyes softened in sympathy. "Take it from me, that only works for a while."

Fortunately, her phone rang before BB could say anything else. Morgan turned away from her inquiring gaze and dug the phone out of her denim sack purse. "Hello?"

"Morgan, it's Mac." Silly her. Too cheap for call display.

Her belly dropped and churned like a river over rocks. "I didn't know about the camera," she blurted.

A three-second silence then, "You thought I'd blame you?"

"Don't you?"

"This is all on me. One of the servers recognized me when I walked past him in the reception hall. But instead of steering clear of you—I was so focused on getting you into that coat check, I didn't think about the consequences." Warmth and concern filled his voice. And regret. He regretted the time with her.

"Oh," she said, then opened the office door so she could get some oxygen. BB's interest had perked up when the word *camera* had entered the conversation. She must know it was Mac. "I'm at work. But thanks for the call." She wanted to hold on to him forever, but she needed to run as fast and as far away from him as she could.

She burst outside and began to pace in a fever of indecision, wishing he'd let her be. Let her go back to being just Morgan Swann.

"I want to come get you," he said. "Take you away somewhere for a few days."

The ache she felt at having to refuse him burned. "I heard you tell Jack that you wouldn't run away from your stalker. You have work to do."

She forced down her joy at the sound of his voice, his

deep, rumbling, sexy-as-hell voice. Then she looked at the work orders still clutched in her hand. "And so do I."

"Going away for a few days will do us good."

Her heart stumbled over the most important word in that sentence. "Us? There is no us. There can't be."

"A few days. A week. Take the time off. You must have read the article, Morgan. The *Courier* knows your real name and where you live and work. Right now, they've got one reporter working the story. Once word gets out about your real name, you'll be swarmed."

She looked around the lot. No unfamiliar cars. No strangers lurking nearby. "They won't find me. I'll move too fast."

"I'll pay your wages for the week," he blurted.

Shock stalled her for two full seconds. "You can't buy my time! I gave you my weekend freely, without strings, without expectations. Because it was *my* time to give you. Just because I'm not one of your usual women doesn't mean I'm for sale."

"Morgan, I didn't—"

"This conversation is over."

She would not be like her mother, time and time again, waiting for some man to rescue her. Morgan *had* to stand on her own two feet, *had* to be in charge of her life.

She stormed back into the office. "If Mac calls looking for me, you don't know where I am."

"Are you sure?" BB stood up, her face full of concern and support. "Of course you are. You're sure of everything."

She wanted to cry, but she was too angry to allow the weakness. She slipped her sunglasses on and faced her friend squarely. "The only thing I'm certain of is that I can't see him right now. He thinks he can ride into my life and sweep me off my feet. He thinks I need to be rescued."

"And nothing could be further from the truth, is that about right? You can outrun these tabloids, you can hide from a swarm of reporters, but you can't outrun yourself."

"Just watch me." She opened the door, but before she could step outside, BB spoke again.

"What about his stalker? What if Jack Carling calls?"

"Jack will get the stalker." She was sure of it. "And Mac wouldn't ask Jack to find me." Or to speak for him. "He'd want to come for me himself. And I will not see him. Understood?" She stared out the door at Bessie and waited.

"If you say so."

Morgan sighed and felt a weight descend on her shoulders. "I'll hide for as long as I need to."

Settled inside Bessie, she cranked the ignition. The rumbling clicks of the diesel brought bone-deep satisfaction.

She *would* bury herself in work.

Days *would* move into weeks, and at some point, thinking of Mac *would* stop hurting.

Right now, she needed to make the shaking stop. She kept her hands in a death grip on the steering wheel and headed out of the lot. She pulled into the traffic flow on the cross street then realized she hadn't read the address on the work order. Checking the rearview and side mirrors, she drew over to the curb to read the paperwork. She waved on a beige car behind her and then checked her street map to find the address she needed.

Just her luck, she had to turn around and get on the

freeway. If she didn't get her head on straight she'd drive in circles all day.

The same beige car pulled in behind her when she hit the on-ramp. Goose bumps stole along her arms, so she slowed and allowed the car to pull ahead of her.

The driver honked and glared, flipping her the finger as she roared past. A blonde woman with spiky short hair, skinny arms and a tight jaw flashed by as Morgan settled into her seat again.

If this was a game of chicken, Bessie could be one mean machine, but if this was hide-and-seek, the blonde could outmaneuver her.

The woman took the next exit. Morgan relaxed her grip on the steering wheel and turned her attention to the road. With any luck, she'd have a long, full day ahead of her. Five minutes later, the blonde was three cars back.

10

AT 5:00 P.M. MAC PACED his den, growled at Rory and roared into the phone at Jack. "What do you mean you don't understand what this guy's up to?" The IT crew had followed a trail of cyber bread crumbs right up to the stalker's door.

Jonathan Lake had used the same Internet service providers to cover his tracks for each attack. Jack sounded as cold as Mac was hot. "No experienced cracker would make this mistake."

"You're saying he *wants* to get caught?" He couldn't see why the stalker would expose himself unless he wanted to divert their attention from some other scheme. They'd tossed that idea around but Jack had covered every base. All Mac's accounts had been moved, changed or closed. His entire life was now behind an impenetrable wall. He glared across the grounds to the back wall and the garden shed. He considered closing off the exit, but it was the only way to escape the grounds if the paparazzi laid siege to the gates. "Put a camera in the shed. If anyone comes and goes through there, we should know about it."

"I did that after the power outage," Jack replied dryly.

"Good." A new thought came to him. "This mistake the cracker made. Maybe it wasn't Lake's idea to do all this in the first place." Maybe he'd been seduced into it. Men did stupid things for beautiful women. His father had been a prime example.

"Wild assumption there, Mac. This guy's likely smarter than you think."

"Then why make an obvious mistake?"

"I'll get back to you on that once we find him. In the meantime, grab a beer, take a swim or do whatever the hell it is you do to let off some steam. You're a mess." He hung up.

Mac tossed his cell phone on the black lounger. He wasn't a mess, he was frantic about Morgan. She wasn't answering her phone and BB refused to tell him where she'd gone. It had taken a lot of convincing to make her admit Morgan had taken three work orders and headed out to do some recoveries.

Cassie's contact at the *Courier* had suddenly stopped talking and she figured it was because they were already following Morgan.

All he could hope was that BB had got through to Morgan and Morgan knew she was being followed.

So why wasn't the bullheaded woman answering her phone?

His gut ached that he'd insulted her. Surely she didn't think he offered to pay— He snapped off the thought and glared at Rory, who'd surprised him by walking into the den.

"When did you start wearing slippers in the house?"

Rory gave him a look he hadn't seen since he was

sixteen and Rory caught him watering down the vodka in his father's liquor cabinet.

"Here's the tabloid you asked for," Rory said, tossing it faceup on the coffee table. He snapped to attention, squared his shoulders and turned smartly to leave the den.

Mac ran both hands down his face. Rubbed until he felt his anger clear some. "Rory, thanks." He got up to get the paper, the third one with no mention of himself or Morgan. She'd be better off if he left her alone. "At least Morgan's free of all this."

"Lucky girl," Rory said and marched out.

Mac had apologized, but voice mail wasn't the same as face-to-face. If she returned his calls, he'd ask her to lunch the way he'd planned and apologize in person. Once this stalker was found, they could pick up where they'd left off.

He blew out a breath, let frustration eat at him.

He could drive past her apartment building to see if it had any security. The irony of the idea didn't escape him.

A victim of a nasty stalking wanting to stalk a woman he barely knew. A woman he genuinely liked. A woman he'd insulted.

"Rory, get your coat. We're going out!"

"Where?" Rory bellowed back from the kitchen.

"To *her* place, where else?"

"'Bout time," Rory roared back. "I'm driving! You'll kill us both with the mood you're in."

AT DUSK, MORGAN TAPPED the steering wheel and bounced in her seat, high on adrenaline as she watched her next target's house. Losing that blonde had given her a rush she hadn't had since she'd last stolen a car. A little backtracking and a sudden turn or two without signaling had taken her to her own neighborhood.

She'd needed nothing more than a phone call to have a garage door open just when she needed it, then closed the second Bessie was hidden inside. She might be living on the straight and narrow, but she still had friends from the old days she could count on for cover. The blonde had been gone when Morgan had exited her old friend's garage.

The radio crackled to life and she snatched it up. "It's about time you picked up. Where have you been?"

"Hanging out with some old friends and laying low."

"He's calling here every half hour," BB said. "And he's burning my ear. Just call the man and get him off my back."

"No can do."

"Now he says the *World Courier* has your real name after all. And they know you work here and where you live."

"So what? I've already lost a tail today. I can take care of myself."

"Stay with me tonight."

"Good idea. I will." She'd swing by her apartment and get some clothes and her own toothbrush first. "I'll call you later. I'm sitting in front of my last recovery for the day and trying to decide if things look okay or not."

"If you're wondering, then it's not okay. I'll send Joe. Wait for him before you do anything."

"Right. Will do." Just because she was high on excitement didn't make her stupid. "Call me back if he's going to be longer than thirty minutes."

"Roger that. Out."

She returned the handset to the cradle and called her

mother while she had a few minutes to talk. If anyone knew how to get over a man, it was Elizabeth Swann.

"Hi, Mom."

"Morgan. I'm glad you called." Her mom's warm tone welcomed her. As adults they were much better friends than they'd been in Morgan's teens. She gave her mom a brief, edited version of the weekend she'd spent with Mac. Still careful about his identity, she only used his nickname.

"I don't know why you don't reel him in, Morgan. He sounds great, and if he's got a good job, you won't have to keep driving that smelly truck and working with those people."

Morgan closed her eyes, drew a breath and counted to three. "Those people are my friends and I'm not going to reel anybody in just so I can quit a job I like."

"Then move on. If this man didn't do it for you, there'll be another one. There always is."

There was a pause, and Morgan could imagine her mother's pursed lips. "Play the field if you want to get over him," Elizabeth advised after a moment. "But wait a few days to see if he calls."

"You still have a spare room?"

"Yes. Are you coming to Miami for a visit?"

She thought about what would happen if reporters followed her. One she could handle, maybe two, but not a swarm. "I'm thinking about it."

"You can stay for as long as you want," her mother said. "In fact, you could move here, get a job. One that doesn't involve danger."

Morgan laughed at the notion. What would she do without her periodic hits of adrenaline? She needed the hunt, the chase, the capture. Those things would fill in for the excitement of a relationship.

It had worked before, it would work again. Look at how much more in charge she felt just by losing that blonde in the car.

"I'll think about it, Mom." She moved the conversation to other things, like Elizabeth's relationship with Ernie.

She had to hand it to her mother. It might have taken seven tries to get it right, but it seemed this marriage was rock solid. Elizabeth was fully engaged in her life with Ernie.

Dusk turned into night as she watched for any sign of activity. Safely cocooned inside Bessie's cab, she waited for Joe, shielded from prying eyes.

In her mind she ran through the real differences between her and Mac. She'd been a streetwise, tough-talking car thief while he'd taken his dad's car keys.

He'd been raised in a mansion with a butler and house-keepers. He'd come to the rescue of a child while Morgan had set out on her own path.

Mac was a rescuer while Morgan refused rescue.

She could and would handle whatever life threw at her. Today's run-in with the blonde reporter was proof. Jack Carling couldn't have done better himself.

Lights inside the house winked on as she watched. The living room, most likely. The glow from a television screen lit up a corner of the window.

The driveway was so littered it was hard to tell if it was used with any regularity. She needed a closer look to be certain.

The lights went out as Joe pulled up. His truck faced hers, headlights blinding in the dark. He climbed down and walked toward her.

"The lights went off," he said, peering through her window.

"Yes." She tried to banish the eyelash image from her mind, but she wasn't sure it was possible. "I haven't seen anyone come or go."

"You're after a pickup truck?"

She nodded. "That garage looks too small. It must be forty or fifty years old." The roof sagged and the door no longer fit squarely.

"Cars were big forty years ago."

"I'll sneak up and take a peek in the side window just to be sure."

"I'll go," he said, and turned away.

She opened Bessie's door. "I'm dressed in dark clothes. You're wearing a white T-shirt." She jumped to the ground, pulling on her gloves as she rounded Bessie's front end.

"Be careful. I'll be right here if you need me."

She nodded.

"Wait," he said.

"What?" she whispered back.

"There aren't any dogs, are there?"

"Not that I've seen or heard and I've been here awhile."

She hunkered down and crept along the sidewalk and then up the driveway. If the truck wasn't here, she could go to BB's, get a good night's sleep and pretend she wasn't yearning for Mac's touch. She kept to the shadows and crouched lower with each step.

The buzz under her skin felt welcome and familiar as she moved. The driveway litter consisted of reasonably fresh takeout boxes and food wrappers. No sound came from inside the house as she peered into the side window of the garage. The truck, just as she'd suspected. A shiny black Chevy four-by-four. Bingo. She grinned, delighted her instincts had been right.

She turned to leave.

"Who the hell are you?" A quiet, tense male voice came from the back porch.

She froze, still in her half crouch. He hadn't turned on a porch light, so he was just as happy as she was with the cover of darkness. Her heart raced with the realization that he didn't want to be seen. A click sounded. From a handgun? Not that she'd heard many, but still, it was best to be safe.

Choice number one was to stand up, tell him the score and take her chances.

Choice number two was to run like hell and hope he couldn't see her well enough to aim properly.

"I'm with Five Aces Towing, here to recover your truck. I've got paperwork." A niggle of precaution caused her to take a runner's stance.

"Repo? Bullshit!" In the shadow of the back stoop, she saw him push at the screen door.

He waved something lethal looking. She sprinted back up the drive toward the street, keeping low.

A thud kicked up the dirt beside her right foot as she ran. Faster. Harder.

Crap!

Her heart thudded and her ears rang as she turned onto the sidewalk and made for Bessie. "He's armed! Shots fired!" she screamed at Joe. Her lungs felt like bellows as she gulped air and ran faster. "Call 9-1-1."

She considered a dive into Bessie's front seat but decided against being a sitting duck. No, she'd use Bessie as a shield. Then she'd deke into a backyard and wait for the police.

She'd give her statement and get the hell home where it was quiet and safe. Feet pounding the pavement, she pushed her legs to go faster, farther.

She listened for sirens and more ominous thuds beside her. "Joe!" she screamed, but couldn't hear a response over her pounding heart. She stopped at a high board fence at the end of the driveway. A dog snarled on the other side, low and menacing.

A chain-link fence surrounded the neighbor's yard. She hopped it and stopped to listen. "Bad dog!" she snapped. The dog whined softly as it padded back and forth on the other side of the fence.

At long last sirens sounded in the distance and she bent over, hands on her knees to catch her breath. Her cell phone vibrated in her back pocket. She flipped it open, hoping to hear Joe's voice.

"Morgan! We have to talk. Where are you?"

"Mac?" She heaved in a breath. "Now's not a good time."

"Do I hear sirens?"

"Gotta go!" The last thing she wanted was Mac to show up. With police scanners screaming that shots had been fired, news crews would show up in moments. Someone would get another picture of them together. This time it would be a credible news report, not just tabloid sensationalism.

She heaved in a couple more deep breaths and listened for activity on the street. A truck fired up, and she heard the sound of splintering wood and then spewing gravel. It was either Joe or the jerk with the gun trying to get away with the pickup. She heard police shouting and tires screeching to a halt.

Damn, now the truck would end up in the police impound.

Her phone rang again. She answered.

"Don't hang up on me! You tell me where you are right now. I can be there in minutes."

"I don't want you here." But she did want him. Here, with her. So he could hold her and tell her she wasn't crazy for doing this job.

Through the phone, she heard a car door open then slam shut. He was on his way to her. He only needed her location and he'd be here. She flashed on the feel of his arms, how he smelled when aroused, the way his chest hair curled around her index finger. She closed her eyes, sucked in a breath.

"I'm at work and I need to go and talk to the police, but I'm fine," she assured him. She tossed the phone gently to the ground on the other side of the fence, then climbed over. Her breath came out with a whoosh. She picked up again. "I have to go now."

"But—"

"But nothing," she interrupted as she walked purposefully along the driveway. Ahead she saw the swirling lights of a police squad car. "This is my job, Mac. This is my life. The life I...like." Did she still like it? She wasn't sure anymore. But she was certain that there was no future for her with Mac. "And Jack's right, I'm not the woman you think I am. I don't need you to rescue me. Goodbye. I won't forget the time we spent together." She disconnected and slipped the phone into her pocket. She wouldn't answer again.

As she approached the police officers, she saw Joe in animated conversation. He turned to her and hugged her tight. "Morgan, thank God you're safe. Are you okay? BB's going to shoot me herself for letting you go up that driveway."

She let Joe hold her a moment so she could get her bearings, then she felt dizzy. He grabbed her as she bent at the waist to keep from fainting. Emergency services checked her over, gave her the all clear so she could make her statement to the police.

Around midnight, Morgan pulled Bessie into her apartment building's parking lot. She'd taken a round-about route home so no one could follow her. Joe had gone to BB's and she figured they'd want their privacy. Besides, at this time of night, she doubted anyone would still be lurking outside her building.

A couple of television news vans had shown up at the scene of the aborted repossession, but she'd kept well away from them, although camera flashes had come from every direction.

The building superintendent didn't like the sight of Bessie and made Morgan park the truck in a back corner so no one could see it from the road. He was a pretentious man, living an unpretentious life, but he had standards, and a tow truck parked in his lot somehow offended him. She supposed he'd be happy if she moved out, but she'd been here longer than he had and she refused to be pushed around.

She climbed down, grabbed her still-warm pizza and shouldered Bessie's door closed. Thank God for all-night pizza joints. Raindrops spattered the pavement as she dashed across the parking lot to the back door of the building, cursing the super for making her park so far away.

She still felt the reaction from the adrenaline of the chase, but it wasn't as much fun as it usually was. Getting shot at destroyed the thrill. Funny how that worked.

As she'd given her statement to the cops, she'd been shaking and freezing cold. Joe had forced her to take his jacket but it hadn't helped much.

She wanted Mac. Needed Mac. His steadiness would calm her. He'd been a rock this weekend when everyone around him had been frantic about the crazy events. He'd never once doubted her, in spite of Jack's obvious suspicions.

Mac didn't even blame her for that photo in the tabloid. He was more worried *for* her. She wanted to tell him that she'd handled far worse things in her life.

Jail for one. Six different dads, for another.

What a fool she was to want the man just because she'd had a fright. She needed to grow a pair, she really did. Pining for Mac's solid reassurance would only lead to a sleepless night. She needed sleep. Dreamless, restful sleep. No more dreams of Mac, no more yearning to feel his body next to hers.

A cup of herbal tea would help. She slid her key into her lock and pushed the apartment door open with her shoulder. A lamp in the living room spilled light onto the floor in a golden circle. The sight warmed and welcomed her, but she hadn't left it on and she still hadn't picked up a timer. She started to back out, frightened again.

A deep voice boomed across the room. "Where the *hell* have you been?"

11

MAC SAT ON MORGAN'S tiny sofa, bristling with anger, fear and relief that she was home, safe and sound.

"How the *hell* did you get in here?" she fired back at him. Her pizza box wobbled while she fumbled with the key. "That wasn't what I wanted to say! Why do I always—" Her distress burst out of her and hit him in the chest.

"Oh God, Morgan, you scared the hell out of me!" Her near-tears expression made him move—*fast*—to get to her.

He rescued the teetering pizza box and slid it onto the kitchen counter then dragged her into his arms, where she belonged. "I got in because Rory has a way with locks."

"Figures," she said through a teeth-chattering smile.

"God, I heard those sirens—" He cut off his own words by covering her lips in a kiss. He could no more hold back his fear than he could walk on water. She let him hold her, let him comfort her, while he assured himself she was uninjured.

"I was scared, Mac. There was a gun. I've seen them before but this time, this time he *used* it."

Mac stiffened, went cold with a mixture of rage and terror.

"What happened, baby? Tell me." *Tell me the bastard's name!*

"I watched this house for hours and figured there was a pickup hidden in an old garage, but I didn't feel right about the place. After dark, I sneaked up the driveway, but he must have seen me because he st-st-started shoo—shooting and I ran. I ran so hard!"

"You got away? He didn't hurt you?" He'd heard the sirens and shouts. The horror of those moments sent a shock to his gut. He held her tighter. "I would have come for you. Why didn't you tell me where you were?"

"I c-c-couldn't. You don't have to rescue me." She looked up at him, her eyes tear-filled, her beautiful face white with fear.

"Those sirens, I thought—I don't know what I thought. I envisioned you on the road, bleeding. Torn up!" He shuddered with the need to hold on to her, to feel every muscle, every curve, to see if she hurt anywhere.

She pulled back, set her hands on either side of his face. "And somehow, in the middle of all that, I decided to take your call? While I was lying in the street?" And there she was, the Morgan he knew, the feisty, cheeky slip of a woman who had stolen his heart.

She smiled, then slid her hands to his shoulders, gave him a reassuring squeeze. "I'm fine."

"Then why are you shaking?"

"That's not me," she said with a gleam in her eye, "that's you."

He chuckled. The lie was in her eyes, in her trembling hands. "Then kiss me and make it stop." He groaned as he pulled her closer. Sweet heaven, she was soft where he was hard and he needed to claim her.

He lifted her and stood while she wrapped her legs around his waist. He scooped her delectable behind higher. With no hall, this was the most compact apartment he'd ever seen. "The bedroom's on the right," she said.

He nudged his way through the door to find a narrow bed jammed into a corner with a single dresser on a side wall. When he set her down he heard springs creak.

She bit her lip. "Tight for space, but we'll manage."

"I like tight." He pulled off her T-shirt, overwhelmed by joy at holding her safely against him.

"The headboard is against an outside wall," she murmured. "We can bang that thing all night and no one will hear."

He laughed, loud and long. "Morgan Swann, I love the way you think."

"So I've heard." She licked her lips as her gaze traveled the length of him and settled on his groin. "I love this part," she murmured. "I love that you're so hard and straining to be free of your underwear. It's like unwrapping the best present I've ever received, Christmas, birthday, whatever. What you have behind this warm cotton is exactly what I need. What I crave. And right now there's nothing in this world I want more than I want you."

The words alone were enough to send the last of his blood to his cock. "Morgan—" He bit off the words. If he said what he felt, he could never take the words back.

The unspoken words zipped away when Morgan tugged down the band of his underwear and took a peek inside. She let the band settle again, exposing the glistening head of his erection, charged for action.

When she raised her eyes to stare into his and her

tongue slicked across her lower lip, he was done for. She knelt and took him into her mouth.

Morgan gave and gave and gave with her mouth, her lips and her tongue. He kept a gentle hand on her lustrous hair, letting the strands of heat wrap around his fingers as she worked him.

Long seductive moments later, his knees went weak from blood loss. His brain hardly functioned. "Sweet woman! I can't stand any more."

She looked up, her eyes feverish and glinting *Come get me.* She wrapped her breasts around his wet engorged shaft.

He stuttered with the incredible sensation of heat and softness encasing him. He rubbed against her soft flesh and groaned.

"You make me wild." Then wilder still as she moved, pumping him.

Unable to take any more, Mac slid to his knees and kissed her mouth. "Enough, Morgan. I need—" He'd never needed a woman the way he needed her.

"There's a pack of condoms in the nightstand," she said.

His inner caveman crowed when he found the box unopened. He would be the first and only man to use them with her.

MAC'S LARGE BODY FOLDED around her like a blanket, hip covering hip, legs covering legs, his shoulder and arm draped across her chest. She drank in his scent, his heat, and felt healed from the ravages of the fear.

"I need to know you're safe and that I'll never hear sirens around you again." His voice, rough with emotion, sated from the loving, rumbled through the air between them. His hips pressed hers, showing his readiness again.

"Oh, Mac." Her heart stuttered with feelings she refused to accept. Infatuation was too small, too easy a word for what she felt. "You make me feel safe, as if we're in the eye of a storm, where it's calm. Everything else is swirling around us, but we're okay."

She turned in his arms, raised her leg to cover his and allowed him to sink into her center in a gentle rocking that soon swept them over the brink.

Too late, she understood that she'd lost another part of herself. He swept hair off her face and grinned down at her. "You feel safe with me, while I feel like I've been picked up and tossed around. I fall back to earth in pieces."

"Don't worry, I'll put you back together."

Mac took up most of the bed, but she didn't mind. He dragged her against his chest and sighed into the pillow. She had exactly what she needed for now—Mac, asleep in her bed, his arms around her.

The clock glowed 3:00 a.m. but sleep eluded her in spite of the loving. Mac had been desperate to hold her and make sure she was all right. He'd skimmed her body countless times as he'd inspected her for injuries.

Wired and edgy, she closed her eyes and relived the fright. Those bullets could have been aimed higher and the outcome very different. She shivered, not from cold, but delayed reaction.

Once the cops had subdued the gunman, they'd discovered he was wanted in three states for violent crimes. She'd stumbled on a fugitive.

The detective who'd arrived shortly after the uniforms told her she'd been lucky. If she hadn't been so quick to hotfoot it out of the drive, he might have dragged her into the house.

She wouldn't have made it out alive.

She couldn't tell Mac what she'd walked into. The gunman turned out to be the deadbeat's cousin. There was no way anyone could have known that his fugitive cousin had used his place as a hideout.

Joe hadn't stuck around long enough to hear about the guy's record. He'd been anxious to see BB, to let her know that he was all right. The man's violent history had to be Morgan's secret. Morgan's nightmare.

She counted Mac's heartbeats, strong and steady until she calmed enough to slide toward sleep.

She slept with her window open a crack for fresh air. Tonight, with spring leaning hard into summer, it was open several inches. She could feel a breeze now, cool on her shoulder, a contrast to Mac's heat.

As she quieted and let her mind drift, she heard an odd noise from outside. It roused her enough to listen harder. The noises continued. Hissing and muffled clatters. She lifted Mac's arm gently then sat up in bed. There it was again, the unmistakable sound of a can hitting the ground and rolling.

She heard feet on pavement, then a car door shut quietly and a vehicle drive off toward the street.

She slipped to the window and held the curtain back so she could peer out.

A second car pulled into the lot and a man climbed out. Moonlight glinted off silver hair. Jack Carling.

Shielding her nakedness with the drape, she slid her window open another couple of inches. "Jack," she called softly.

He froze, looked up. "Morgan?"

"Did you see that car leave?"

"Yes, why?"

"I've got a bad feeling. What color was it?"

"Tan."

"Or closer to beige?"

"Sure." He nodded.

"Check Bessie for me, will you?"

Suddenly, Mac's solid body was at her back, bringing welcome heat and a sense of strength she could lean on. "Jack's out there. Now, why would he be watching my apartment building?" She put some starch in her voice to hide her apprehension at what he might find.

Mac cleared his throat.

"Hmm," she said. "Cat got your tongue?"

"Don't get riled, Morgan. After what I heard earlier, it's a wonder I haven't dragged you back to my place kicking and screaming."

Jack spun to face her window again. "Get Mac and some clothes, Morgan," he called softly. "You can't stay here."

She tilted her head back to catch Mac's eye. "Your stalker must have followed you." She shuddered. "Tell me he did not sit under my bedroom window while we made love."

"I'd like to tell you that, but…" He trailed away, letting her come to her own conclusion.

"Do you think he heard us?" *Ugh!* Maybe he used a listening device that caught every sigh and moan. Each whispered word. This was far worse than the coat check booth. Here, they'd let all their passion out in long drawn-out sighs, moans, and yes, even a scream or two. She flushed.

The creepiest, crawliest feeling squeaked along her nerve endings. She shook it off in another shudder. She had to put her mind into gear.

His large palms gripped her shoulders and tugged her back against him.

"No one knows what's in this person's mind. They're sick, whoever they are."

"I'm officially creeped out more than I've ever been, and I've seen some weird stuff."

"We're out of here, Morgan." He spun and grabbed his clothes from the dresser, where she'd laid them.

She shivered with the cold chill of fear and ran her hands up her arms in response. "You'll get no argument from me."

"I won't hear one." He pulled on his slacks and shirt while she dug out her backpack from the bottom of her closet.

The rasping buzz of the intercom sounded. "That must be Jack. Can you let him in?" She stuffed a weekend's worth of clothes into her backpack then hit the bathroom next and scooped up toiletries as Mac let Jack into the building. "I'm not leaving without fresh clothes and my own toothbrush."

From the living room, she heard, "They hit her truck, Mac. That's all."

"That's all? That's everything!" she cried. She zipped up her pack and shouldered past the two men to dash down the back stairs.

"Morgan," Mac growled, "get back here!"

She moved faster, slammed open the stairwell door and headed down. Quick, quick.

Mac and a muttering Jack followed close behind her, but she was faster and put her lead to good use.

At the bottom, she dashed outside and headed straight for Bessie. She skidded to a halt in front of her truck and touched tacky paint. The windshield was completely covered. The truck couldn't be driven. Except for the spray paint can that had bounced under the truck, there was no trail left by the perpetrator.

Bessie had been vandalized: spray-painted with the word *whore* across the windshield and all the doors. Another word that began with a *C* was written along the truck bed. "I guess someone figured out that I'm the one in the photo with you."

Morgan put her head down on her forearm as she peered inside the truck. No damage that she could see.

Mac stood behind her. "Your arm will be covered in paint."

She didn't care. "This isn't the first time a Five Aces truck has been vandalized," she said in a reasonable tone. "I have to see if she'll start." She unlocked the door, went to open it.

"No!" Jack stopped her. "There's no telling what's been done. You two go home. I'll call the police and deal with this."

"But I can't go home, can I?" she said. "They know where I live now." She looked up at her dark bedroom window. "But this might not be Mac's stalker, right? This could be about my job. Maybe I pissed somebody off enough that they want to get back at me."

Mac drew her into his protective arms. "Regardless of where this threat has come from, I need to get you away from here. Let's go home where you'll be safe."

Exhaustion licked at her. She waited for a pump of adrenaline but came up empty. "I heard the hiss of the spray can. I heard it hit the ground and roll."

He stood in stubborn silence.

"Okay," she said, leaning into him, too tired to resist him and his offer of quiet in the storm. "Take me to your place. But just for the night. I'll borrow another truck for work tomorrow."

She meant the words to sound defiant, but they came out tired and defeated instead. Another look at Bessie convinced her she was caught up in this vendetta against Mac. The words were so...personal. And ugly.

Not like the gunman earlier. He hadn't shot at a woman named Morgan Swann. He'd shot at a stranger nosing around the property. He'd fired because he was on the run and didn't want to be captured. When she'd said she was there for the truck, he reacted in his own violent way.

None of what had happened to her earlier had been personal. Not like this.

Her wild run down the street and over the fence was etched into her mind. The unreality of the guy on the porch, with the gun in his hand, the dull whap of the bullet kicking up dirt beside her—all of it ran before her eyes in slo-mo. Oh, God. She'd been so scared.

"Take me home, Mac."

In the car, she replayed the events of the evening for Jack's sake. When she finished, he blew out a breath. "You kept your head, Morgan. Which is more than a lot of people could do. You should be proud of yourself." The respect that laced through his response would have warmed her this morning, but now, she was too tired to care.

"How did you know the car was beige?"

She was also too tired to lie. "I saw it earlier today. Three times. I lost her. I thought I was so smart, handling everything myself. I should have laid low all day." But the lure of the adrenaline rush had overpowered her.

Mac held her close, but didn't speak. Didn't even remind her that he'd warned her the reporter was after her.

"You tried to tell me, Mac, but I was too stubborn to hear you."

"The beige car didn't belong to the *Courier* reporter. A reporter wouldn't vandalize your truck." Jack blew out a breath.

Mac's voice sounded hollow. "It must be my stalker."

12

TUESDAY MORNING AND Morgan woke slowly. Birdsong filtered into her consciousness, followed by the faint light that edged the draperies. She peeped open one eye, then stretched as far as she could to feel for Mac.

The king-size bed was cool where she touched. He'd been gone for some time. She rolled to the middle and stared at the ceiling. She was locked behind the gates of Mac's estate like a fugitive when she'd done nothing wrong.

She spied a tray on a side table that held the makings for her first cup of coffee. Mac. How considerate he was, as a host and a lover. He'd taken care of every imaginable need the night before. He'd made love to her, made her feel safe, brought her here, but mostly he'd supported her in ways she'd denied she needed until she was too tired to be stubborn.

Her real trouble was that she'd fallen in love with an impossible man.

But as soon as it was safe to get out from behind these walls, she was gone.

She checked the time. Eight forty-five and BB would

be at her desk. The drivers would be on the road. She called the office.

"Hi, it's me."

"Morgan! Where are you?"

"You sitting down?"

"What's up?"

She told BB about Bessie being vandalized. "Don't worry, Mac's seen to it. She'll be clean and shiny in a couple of days. The old girl was due for some TLC anyway."

"Are you all right?"

"Yes, last night just shook me up some." She squeezed her eyes shut. "No, change that. I've made a huge mistake."

"What are we talking about here?"

"I love him, BB. I do, and I don't know how to walk away."

"Oh, girlfriend, I'm so sorry. But you can't leave. Turn on the television."

In the sitting area she found the local news station. The street in front of Mac's gates was full of people, vans, and cameras. It was bad enough that the stalker had found her at home. Now this. "Oh, no! What do they want?"

"To get a shot of you, I guess. Stay inside, wait for this to blow over. And—" her voice dropped, laden with caution "—you'd better not come to work for a while."

Her belly dropped as the seriousness of her situation hit. "Am I fired?"

BB hesitated while Morgan sank to the sofa in fear. "Of course not, but we can't operate effectively if people watch our every move. Let's give it a couple of weeks."

After this mess, Mac would be glad to be rid of her. If she was trapped behind the gates, so was he.

There were two things she'd never wanted to lose during this time with Mac. One was her heart, the other was her job.

They were both lost.

Her life was in tatters again, just the way it had been with Johnny DeLongo. "BB, you'll talk to your uncle for me, won't you?"

"I've already told him you need time off to visit your mother. That might not be a bad idea, Morgan. These reporters will move on before they can follow the trail from Mrs. Swann to whatever her name is now." BB chuckled and brought her usual wry humor into the situation. "Will she let you stay with her?"

"She's already invited me. And for once, having all those surnames will be helpful." She'd consider Elizabeth's invitation. She could find work that wasn't dangerous. It was sunny in Florida. There were palm trees. And if anyone knew the cure for a broken heart, it was Elizabeth.

"It isn't right that you can be held hostage this way," BB said. "Last time I checked this was America. You should be free to walk the streets and go to work just like anyone else. You haven't done anything wrong!"

That didn't seem to matter a whit to the crowd at the gates. "Mac's trapped in here, too." The swarm of reporters had nothing to do with his stalker and everything to do with Morgan.

She dropped her head into her hands and groaned with the weight of her mistakes, starting with buying those tabloids. She'd been one of the people who'd clamored for any bit of gossip about the handsome Kingston McRae. "This makes me feel sorry for the celebrities they love to harass."

"Don't kid yourself. Some of those celebrities use the

tabloids to keep their profile high. Not to mention selling photos of their own children for profit. Talk about twisted." BB snorted. "What some people do astounds me."

Morgan agreed and consoled herself that most of the famous women and wannabes on Mac's arm were for public consumption. By agreement, of course. "Mac's PR people arrange for a lot of his public dates, the movie premieres, that kind of thing. The actresses are happy to have a famous escort, especially if they want their actual private life private."

"Sure, makes sense. But what about Mac? What's he keeping private?"

"Up to now? Charity work and a private business program he oversees." She couldn't betray a confidence and explain the mentoring program. "I hope I haven't exposed him to much ridicule."

She promised BB to keep in touch and said goodbye. In the meantime she had no job to go to. Miami looked better by the minute.

She wasn't sure what she could have done differently over these past few days. She'd tried going back to work, tried getting Mac out of her head and her heart, but in the end, she'd failed at all of it. So much for handling her problems herself—she'd only created more!

She pulled on some clothes and stepped out into the hall.

Raised voices came from Mac's office. Probably Mac and Jack, going at it over the stalker again. Jack's frustration with his team rose daily. Mac was more patient, but he felt the strain of being locked in. Great sex was marvelous, but in the wee hours he'd mentioned going out to dinner.

In public.

Like a date.

She'd done a long, slow slide down his body, taken him into her mouth and put the idea of a public outing out of his head.

The whole idea gave her the hives. If they were seen as a couple, life would never go back to normal. Not for her.

She'd be marked as one of those weird people that popped up on the arm of a celebrity, got dumped, then disappeared again. Sometimes she wondered what the heck they were thinking getting involved with someone famous. Maybe it was the money, the fame, the attention. Their own fifteen minutes.

And maybe, just maybe, it had nothing to do with being smart and everything to do with feelings.

She shut that thought down. Hard.

Her relationship with Mac could never go public. She'd make sure of that. She didn't want to play with that fantasy again.

Mac's office door was open, and just as Morgan suspected, a frustrated Jack Carling stood inside glaring at Mac, who was silhouetted by the stream of sunshine at the window.

"Good morning," she said, breezily ignoring the testosterone-laced silence. "I called BB and she told me to turn on the television." She nodded toward the security monitors that showed pockets of three and four people standing around, ready to pounce, cameras at the ready.

Jack spun when she entered, none too happy with her arrival.

He held up a copy of the *World Courier*. He'd scrunched the flimsy newsprint up so hard she couldn't make out the headlines.

Her belly sank at the expression on Mac's face. She wanted, badly, to rub her achy gut, but she took the paper from Jack instead.

The muscle in Mac's jaw jumped. Never a good sign. She stared at him. She didn't want to look at what must be another damning photo. "There's an article and more pictures of you. From last night." His tic worked faster and he raised his voice. "You have to quit that job!"

"That *job* is all I've got!" The thud of the bullets in the dirt by her feet rattled through her skull.

"He warned me off, Mac. He didn't want to kill me." The words of reassurance cost her big-time.

"Oh, God," he mumbled, and drew her into his arms. She went stiff at his rough grasp, but let him hold her. He spoke against her ear and neck. "It was bad enough that you shook and cried in my arms, but to see you run for your life—I can't take it."

She used to love the thrill of the chase, the hunt, outwitting men and finding people who didn't want to be found.

Jack pointed to the crinkled pages still in her hand, forgotten. She placed the tabloid on Mac's desk and smoothed the front page. "Oh, I see." Mac was right—she *was* running for her life. Her grimace was gruesome, her boobs looked about to pop out of her T-shirt, and her shorts had ridden high on her butt. She had no idea adrenaline could look like that. Ugly, really, really ugly.

This is who Kingston McRae is slumming with these days. Morgan Swann, fleeing bullets, sirens blaring on a quiet street. Why is our favorite bachelor hanging with a woman like this?

THE HEADLINE MADE IT look as if the cops were chasing her. It was a vicious slant on the real events.

"I was so smug about losing the blonde in that beige beater." Twice in the day she'd taken vehicles to the impound lot. "I must have picked up a tail from a real reporter afterward."

But she had to admit, she looked pretty wild in the photos. Nothing at all like the beauties he was usually seen with. "Oh, yay! More pictures on page two." It wasn't as much fun to turn the page when she was the subject of the story.

The next photo showed her bent over at the waist, clutching her knees as she tried to catch her breath. She remembered that moment. It had felt like someone had knocked all the oxygen from her lungs. The back side of her shorts looked like something out of a porn flick. If it hadn't been dark outside, the photo would have had a fade-out to obscure her private parts. As it was, she seemed to be offering herself. The only thing worse would have been a front-page spread, but the photo was too lurid to be displayed in grocery stores.

"They make me look like I'm drunk and ready to pass out." Or worse. "And that Joe—"

"I don't care about the pictures, or the comment on slumming," Mac said. "It's too ridiculous! We'll sue for libel. They've got no right to say you've been to jail."

She swallowed hard and skimmed the article. "Technically it was juvie," she said softly. "But those records are supposed to be sealed. I was fifteen." She refused to look at Mac. She *had* mentioned it, but he'd fixated on the number of stepfathers in her life and she had let the moment for truth pass.

Jack swore. "I should have known."

"Guess your security team's not so hotshot after all," Morgan quipped.

"So, it's true?" Mac murmured with a frown.

She shrugged. Truth time. It had to come out sooner or later. "Yes. I mentioned it to you, but you assumed I was busted for joyriding. The conversation moved on."

She raised her chin and ignored Jack's narrowed gaze. "I'm past being defensive about the mistakes I've made." What was important were the lessons she'd learned from those years.

And one of those lessons rolled through her right now. Charmed! Kingston McRae had charmed her just as easily as Johnny DeLongo had. Both times, she'd taken a chance on men and she was the one who ended up with her life in tatters.

Damn! Why couldn't she learn to steer clear of charmers?

Mac hadn't set out to ruin her life or use her the way Johnny had, but the devastation was the same. Except this time, her mother was there for her, unlike in her teens.

She walked past Jack and around Mac's desk to the window. From here she could see the roof of the portico and the drive that led down to his estate gates.

"If it wasn't joyriding, then what was it?" Jack asked.

"I stole cars for a car theft ring," she said baldly. "And for a time it was a hell of a lot of fun. Thrilling, even. For what it's worth, I'm sorry I wasn't up-front about it, but I tried." She shrugged and crossed her arms under her breasts as she leaned against the window frame. "I understood exactly what I was doing, and I knew the cars would never get back to their owners." She shrugged again. "I figured most of the rich dudes had insurance."

"Rich dudes?" It was Mac, sounding hollow.

Mac was seeing the real her. She decided she might as well dig the hole she was in deeper. "My mother figured it would teach me a lesson for being stupid about men. She refused to cooperate with any offers to send me for counseling instead of incarcerating me."

"What kind of lessons could a teenage girl learn in jail?"

"Not to depend on anyone to get me out of trouble."

"Which in your mind equates with being rescued." Mac's sharp voice stung.

"It also gave my mother time without me around to snag her next husband." This was it, the end. Now that Mac saw the real Morgan Swann, she could go back to her own life. Or what was left of it.

"What facility were you in?" It was Jack.

"So you can check my story? See how bad I really was?" When he didn't respond, she went on. "I had a judge who knew the gang used young teenage girls. He offered me a place in a halfway house after he talked to my mother. I got the help I needed and have stayed out of trouble ever since."

"Did you go back home afterward?"

She shrugged. "I did a couple of college semesters, but when my mother divorced that husband, I left and struck out on my own." The memory of her first glimpse of Kingston McRae in a tabloid washed over her. She'd been lonely, broke and afraid of sliding back into crime. The way she'd latched onto his image as some kind of lynchpin or life-saving ring had been peculiar, but it had helped at the time.

Not now.

She wasn't that young woman anymore. This time she

could go to her mother for help. She had BB to lean on, even Joe and the other drivers.

Mac shook his head. "You've been on your own ever since? You were what? Eighteen?" In the window she caught his expression of sympathy. He shook his head. "Man, I thought I had it rough."

His expression stung her pride. "Keep your pity, Mac. A lot of kids had it worse than me. I paid my debt, got on the right side of the law and stayed there. I'm honest, dedicated and have my priorities in order." Her declaration silenced the men, until Jack crossed his arms over his chest.

Great. A speech.

"Spit it out, Jack," she forestalled him. "You want me gone, so I'll go. I'll never bother Mac again." She moved quickly, afraid her eyes might overflow.

Stupidly, she'd fallen for Mac's charm and sophistication. He hadn't set out to ruin her life, to take her job, to break her heart. She was the one who'd allowed it, even when she'd known better.

Only an impulsive fool ignored everything they'd learned.

She took three steps.

Mac reached out so quickly she couldn't dodge him when he took her arm. "You're not going anywhere. Not without me. We'll go wherever you like. A resort? Canada? Europe?"

She shook off his hand, her heart cracking at the concern in his voice. But she'd caused enough trouble. "I can take care of myself." She was used to it. "In fact, I prefer to."

13

"MORGAN, DON'T TAKE this on yourself," Mac said. "Bessie was spray-painted because of the first photo. I was the one who behaved like a Neanderthal, the one who dragged you into that coat check. I didn't care who saw us! I didn't think about anything but getting you alone. I'm the one who knows better."

She blinked, trying hard not to listen, not to believe.

He lowered his voice and leaned in close. "I wanted you so badly, I didn't care that we could be seen. I still want you that way. That much."

She couldn't look away from him. Couldn't move, couldn't think.

"I want to make this right." His voice was rough, needy.

Hearing him like that made her back down, less ready to run for her life. He had hold of her heart again and he knew it.

Oh, crap.

With an effort that cost her dearly, she gathered her wits for one last attempt to break free. "I have a place I can go where no one will find me. You don't have to worry." She reached her hand up to his cheek, his bristly skin warm against her palm.

"Take care of yourself," she said, struggling to hold on to reason and logic. What she wouldn't give to enjoy a getaway with Mac. Somewhere exciting with palm trees and icy drinks in martini glasses. She bit back a sigh, seduced by the images. "I can't go with you. I've got my work, the youth center's open house is coming up. I've shirked my responsibilities there for long enough." A small lie about her job couldn't hurt at this point. If he knew her position at Five Aces was tenuous, he'd insist on helping her. He'd understand about her volunteer work—he was a mentor himself.

"Please understand, Mac. This is for the best." Florida beckoned. She would hide at her mom's place until this blew over. They could reconnect. Elizabeth had reached out when Morgan needed her.

Jack cleared his throat, startling them out of their mental tango. "You'll need protection when you leave," he said to Morgan with a sharp nod. Was that admiration she read in his gaze?

He reached for his phone but Mac stopped him with an impatient wave of his hand.

"Morgan's not going anywhere without me." Mac held out his phone. "Call and make this right at Five Aces, then we'll order some clothes for you and we'll head for the airport. The youth center will have to manage without you."

Pride came to her rescue. She would not be swept away. She would not be *charmed*. She would not be clothed, not when she had perfectly good clothes in her bedroom closet at home.

"You don't understand. My life isn't your life. My life is work, work, more work and then I volunteer to work.

Get it?" He had to understand what he was asking of her. Elizabeth had depended on men her whole life. Morgan would be damned if she did it, too. "If I need clothes I wait for end-of-season sales and hit the stores then. I don't have designer labels delivered to my house to pick and choose from." She held up her hands. "These aren't manicured for a reason, Mac. I use them."

His face went thunder dark. "I want to keep you safe. The stalker knows where you live and work. To hell with the paparazzi. It's the stalker I'm worried about."

"I'll move away. The stalker wants me gone, so I'll go. Long term, all this will be forgotten."

"Will I be forgotten?" His voice went deep with earthy urgency. She saw heated memories flash in his eyes and melted.

Rory stepped into the room, frazzled and shaken. "I just found this in with the mail!" He held up a brown envelope with no name or address on the front.

Jack inspected the envelope before gingerly opening it, careful to handle the paper with tissue so he wouldn't smudge any fingerprints.

A photo slid out with scrawled letters in red across it. The image was different from the *Courier*'s. This picture had been shot from another angle.

"Someone else was there," she said. "Another camera." She glanced at Jack, who was glaring at Mac.

Get rid of the bitch.

"The writing's similar to what's on your truck."

"We're out of here," Mac said. "We'll get clothes when we land."

Jack frowned. "I've got to advise against leaving, Mac. Remember the first photos were of you disembarking from the jet. Whoever this is knows where you keep the jet and may know your pilot's name."

Morgan felt a trickle of fear slither down her back. "This is a nightmare," she said, "and I want to wake up now." Mac enfolded her in his arms. She went into them without protest and took comfort in his strength and familiar scent. She had to stop this! She had to stop leaning on him.

And she would, soon. When all this was over, she'd walk away and lick her wounds in private.

"When you upgraded the security, did you install a camera by the mailbox at the gate?"

"I asked for cameras to cover both directions." He hurried to a monitor, keyed in come commands on the keyboard.

Jack and Rory swore in tandem at what they saw on-screen.

"They mounted one fixed camera six feet above the mailbox and aimed it at the entrance. Unless the person walked up from the direction of the gate, we wouldn't get a shot of them." He sagged in defeat. "Damn it, I should have made sure they installed a pair of roving cameras. I should have seen to this myself."

His phone rang, breaking off anything Mac might have said. Jack answered and listened a moment. "Good work. I'm on my way over. Wait for me." He flipped his phone closed and grinned wide.

"What's up?"

"Jonathan Lake is a real person. A college kid."

Mac frowned. "Old enough to understand what he's doing is illegal."

"What's the connection to Mac?" Morgan asked.

"Jonathan Lake is Lila Markham's younger brother."

"You dated her about five months ago," Morgan broke in, excited. "The *Courier* said for weeks that this was it for Kingston McRae. They said you'd never resist Lila's charms, because all of her costars had fallen for her." Morgan remembered feeling sad that he might actually be in love with the woman. She'd never seemed right for him.

Another of Rory's earthy curses exploded into the room. "Lila! Of course! She wanted to befriend Lindsay. And she spent a lot of time with me when we remodeled the kitchen. She gave me excellent suggestions and came over many times when Mac was out." He clenched his hands into fists so tight his knobby knuckles went white. "I gave her ample opportunity to learn whatever she wanted about the running of the house. She could have slipped into the office at any time, gone anywhere! How could I be so gullible?"

Morgan crowed. "I knew she was wrong for you! I just knew it!" Her outburst echoed in the silence after Rory's confession.

"Okay, okay! I'm sorry, but I had a crush on Mac for years," she confessed, then clarified, "I mean, on the Kingston McRae who showed up in the tabloids." Totally different men as far as she was now concerned.

"A crush?"

She fanned out her fingers. "Totally over it!"

Rory pursed his lips, while Jack darted a derisive glance at the ceiling. Mac grinned. "Over it? I hope not."

"Oh, you know what I mean." She waved her hands. "It was a silly crush that fed some fantasies. That's all."

Mac grinned. "You can tell me about your fantasies later."

She flushed, a victim of her impulsive tongue again, and faced the men. Two of them looked everywhere but at her, while Mac beamed as if he'd found a pot of gold.

He snapped his fingers. "That's why you took so long to get the Morgan hooked up that first time. You were dawdling, hoping to what? Meet me? Admit it, Morgan."

"Can we get back to your scorned woman? Please? She's the one who messed you up, not me."

"That's a matter of opinion," Mac murmured.

"Right, Lila," Jack said. "Why would her brother hack into Mac's computer system? Why mess with him? Did Lila go cry on his shoulder? Does he have a history of this kind of thing?" He called his team to ask those questions and more.

By the time Jack Carling was through with Jonathan Lake he'd be expelled from college at the least and jailed at the worst. She felt a spear of compassion for Lila's brother. Family dynamics might have been part of his decision and there was no telling what Jack had planned for Lila.

Mac stared at Morgan until she shifted warily. "What?"

"You wanted me before you got here." The intensity of his gaze narrowed on her face, her eyes, her soul.

Jack took his phone call into the hall and Rory scuttled out after him.

She rocked back on her heels and shoved her hands in her pockets. "So, what if I did? It wasn't anything *real*. It was a silly, long-distance crush." Played out between the pages of a trash-talking tabloid.

"What about now?"

"What *about* now?" She pretended he wasn't mining for information. Pretended she didn't care if he was.

"Is this just a crush for you? Are you living out a fantasy? Is it the 'rich dude' thing?"

"In a way, I wish it was." She patted her heart. "This is…infatuation. We just have it at the same time."

"We both have it. And?"

"It will last as long as it lasts. Can we agree to let it play out in private? I don't want to be exposed to the circus at the gates any more than I already have been."

He nodded. "Good. I want to see where this is going, too. I'm sorry about the circus and your job. I'm sorry about the vandalism to Bessie, and that you can't go home if you want to. If I'd ignored my interest in you, none of this would have happened."

"We wouldn't know each other. I wouldn't have met Lindsay, or Rory, for that matter." She'd never have glimpsed life on this side of the gates.

He leaned against the window, arms crossed over his chest. His large, brawny chest that she loved to snuggle into.

She didn't want to have this conversation, not while he was distracted by Jack and all the Lila Markham business. "So what about Lila, Mac? Did she have strong feelings for you? You must have had some hint."

"I brushed it off. It was a PR thing as far as I was concerned. I was surprised when she wanted to take it further. And then when she tried to insinuate her way into my life through Rory and Lindsay, I ended it."

Jack slipped back into the room. "I'm on my way to Lila's hotel now. Did you know she wrangled an invitation to the wedding?"

"I didn't see her there. I would have noticed."

"If she dyed and cut her hair? She's a redhead, with long hair as I recall, but the woman Morgan saw following her was a blonde with short hair."

"Damn, she must have changed her face or something." His eyes went stormy. "If I'd paid more attention to the wedding guests, we might have avoided a lot of trouble." He frowned. "But I saw the list—how did I miss Lila's name?"

"She was a last-minute addition," Jack told him. "I doubt even Lindsay recognized her."

"Lindsay was too excited, anyway, and you never told her about a stalker," Morgan added.

Abruptly, Mac straightened, looked fierce. "I'm going with you."

"What about the brother?" Morgan asked Jack.

"The campus police are talking to Jonathan Lake. As far as we can tell he didn't have time to warn his sister we're on to her."

"I want the whole thing kept quiet," Mac said. He wasn't out to destroy anyone's life; he just wanted his own peace of mind back. "I didn't care enough to ask about her family. I never knew she had a brother."

"Until Morgan, the women you saw were conveniences," Jack reminded him. "They all knew that and used the exposure to advance their own careers. Don't beat yourself up."

Obviously, Lila had been hurt. Either that, or she'd misunderstood. He should have seen her interest, deflected it gently instead of leaving without a backward glance.

Morgan looked curious. "How can you get away without the crowd following you?"

"My father installed a secret door in the garden shed in the back wall. It's hidden and rarely used." He drew her into his arms for a kiss. He needed the feel of her, the warmth and reassurance that she'd wait for him. She kissed him back with tremulous lips and looked up at him, one perfect eyebrow raised in question.

"My father used the secret exit to sneak out to see

his various mistresses. My mother used it to have liquor delivered without the embarrassment of having it come through the front gate on a daily basis."

"Oh, Mac, I'm sorry."

He shrugged off the ancient hurt. "I'll talk to Lila at the hotel."

"You want to help her?"

"If I can." He motioned to Jack to lead the way and bussed Morgan quickly on the cheek. "Wait here till I get back. If we can't sort through this mess, we'll go away together. It'll be fun, you'll see."

"Fun, wow." Quiet determination flashed in her eyes, frightening him.

"Morgan, promise you'll stay put."

She kissed him quickly on the lips. "Go." She shoved him away playfully.

He followed Jack out the office door, unhappy she'd avoided that promise, but the chance to finish this once and for all was powerful.

As soon as they were safely in the car Jack had had delivered to the hidden entrance, Mac shot his friend a glance. "What do you think of her?"

"Lila's over the edge and you'd best let the law handle her. She deserves jail time for all she's done to you and to Morgan."

"I'm not talking about Lila. I'll see what she needs when I get to her hotel."

Jack stared out the passenger-side window, his jaw flexed. "Why the hell do you pay me? You never listen!"

"What do you think of Morgan?"

Jack rubbed his face. "Why?"

"I like her, Jack. She's funny and smart and she hasn't asked for a damn thing from me. She's different. And I need different right now. I'm so sick of stick women who want to advance their own agendas.

"Morgan's grown on me. I like that she's kept her head through most of this. I like that she confessed about the car theft ring. She's proud, tough. She had to be tough from her history. Juvenile Hall at fifteen was a bad break, but at least the judge got her out before any real harm was done. Watching her mother depend on men that way would have left a mark, though."

"Don't let Morgan hear that sympathy in your voice. She'll take it as pity and—"

"Break my nose," Jack agreed.

"If anything had happened to Morgan when that guy shot at her, I don't know what I'd do. But it wouldn't be pretty."

"I'd be there, too. Just the two of us. He wouldn't know what hit him." Jack's tone spoke volumes.

"When we get to Lila's, let me speak with her alone," Mac said. Half his mind had stayed behind with Morgan. "Maybe Morgan should have come with us. Just so I could keep an eye on her myself."

"She's better off behind the gates. You can take her wherever you want to go when we get back. For now, let's focus on Lila. When we've dealt with her, I'll look into Morgan's past. A complete file, no stone unturned kind of thing."

"What's the point now?"

"If I can have her record expunged, I'll do it."

"Thanks, but make sure to ask her first."

The cross street held a phalanx of reporters' cars parked along the curb. His mood lightened when he and Jack drove past undetected. "At least we don't have to outrun them," he said.

The moment they arrived in the hotel lobby, the

concierge called the general manager to meet them. He escorted them to Lila's door and tapped lightly.

When there was no response, he used his master key to unlock the suite, then stepped aside to let them enter alone. Lila was gone, but her belongings were strewn about the rooms. "There's the dress she wore to the wedding. And a makeup case with a prosthetic nose."

Jack slipped on gloves, passed a pair to Mac. "She planned this well in advance."

"There's a file folder on the desk by her laptop." Jack flipped open the file and read the top sheet, then looked further through the sheaf of papers. "Copies of your receipts, spreadsheets from your accounting program, passwords, codes. Everything baby brother needed to attack you where it hurt."

On an end table beside the sofa Mac spied a family photo album. He opened to the first page and his stomach turned. "Look at this," he said, waving Jack over to see.

Photographs of Mac and Lila, smiling and happy in places they'd never visited. The next few pages were of them dressed in wedding clothes. "She's sicker than we thought," Mac said quietly, stunned by her level of obsession.

Jack whistled. "These are composites she created from other photos according to her fantasies." He turned another page. "Here she's on the cover of a women's magazine, pregnant. Look at the date."

Mac felt a chill down his spine. "She's lived out the next five years."

He continued to flip pages. There were more pregnancy pictures than anything else. Clearly, she had plans.

"Wonder if she wants a boy or a girl?"

"As if I'd want her to mother my children." An image of Morgan pregnant and happy slipped like silk through his mind. He shuddered at the photo album and closed it with a snap. "Makes you wonder what she had planned for the sixth year."

Jack stared at him, frowning.

"Divorce?" Mac suggested hopefully.

"Or widowhood," Jack replied darkly.

Mac checked the bedroom closet. "The rest of her clothes are here."

"I wonder where she went?"

In the short silence, Mac's stomach turned. "The house!" He ran out, headed for the elevator at a dead run. Jack kept up while he opened his phone.

"She won't get in, Mac. Rory's got the gates on manual. Lila will never—"

Mac cut him off. "I remember Lindsay telling her about the garden shed when they were swapping stories. Lindsay had a boyfriend Rory didn't like and she told Lila about sneaking out to see him." That had been the first time he'd had an inkling that her befriending Rory and Lindsay was a deliberate move to feel included in his life.

Mac felt a trickle of sweat run down his neck. "Morgan and Rory are sitting ducks. If she had full run of the house, she could have a copy of the key for the hidden door. It won't matter that the gates are on manual."

"Morgan's not answering," Jack said. "I'll try the land line in Rory's room."

"If he doesn't answer, try the one for the house. He could be watching television."

Mac bit back a growl of frustration when the elevator stopped for passengers.

An obsessed madwoman was on the loose—and aimed at two people he loved.

14

MORGAN PEEKED INTO the den to check that Rory was still in his lounger, beer in hand. His feet were crossed at the ankles on the footrest. Nothing had changed at the front gates, so he'd decided to settle in for his regular afternoon talk shows.

He seemed engrossed and relaxed for the first time since delivering the photos from Lila Markham.

She tightened her grip on her backpack and turned to leave, grateful Mac had told her about the secret door.

Her phone rang, and she fumbled it out of her denim bag.

"Aren't you going to answer that?"

"No." She shut it off and straightened as he turned in his chair and caught sight of her backpack.

"Where are you going?"

"Where no one can find me. I need to be gone before Mac returns, so stay out of it."

He reached for the phone on his side table.

She walked to it, slipped her hand over his and pushed the handset back down into the cradle. "Don't call him. It's best this way."

If Mac learned she'd gone to the airport he'd be in

the seat next to hers on the flight to Miami. She wasn't stupid.

What Mac wanted, Mac got.

The wealthy could count on people to bend rules for them, on favors being repaid, on money making things happen.

In a battle of wills, though, Morgan was a powerhouse and she knew it. She kept her face stern, her eyes pleading. She wasn't Elizabeth Swann's daughter for nothing! After a long moment, Rory nodded and released the phone.

"Mac will want to know I can bounce back from this, so I need you to convince him I'm fine. Will you do that, Rory?"

He harrumphed, but nodded. It was all she'd get, but it was better than nothing.

She wasn't sure of her ability to land on her feet this time, so convincing Rory helped her convince herself. "Life has a way of knocking you back when you move into social spheres where you don't belong. I'll deal with it, I promise."

"That's ridiculous! Mac will be furious with me if I allow you to sneak off." He moved his chair to upright and stood. "He cares deeply for you."

The jab about Mac's feelings nearly did her in, but she saw through the old sailor anyway. "You can't con me. He won't blame you for *my* decision. Mac's not like that." He would more likely blame himself and think she didn't trust him to keep her safe.

Rory got a cagey look in his eye, so she cut him off before he said anything more. "What part of *stay out of it* don't you get?" she snapped. "I care for him, too, but I can't be here when he gets back."

He frowned and opened his mouth to argue, but she

forged ahead, needing him to understand. "It's better for me to move on while the memories are good. I couldn't take it if he tired of me." *Like all the others.*

Rory narrowed his gaze and ire showed in his eyes. "You've got him all wrong. I know him like my own son, and he—"

"I won't be another Lila. Left behind, desperate. I won't do that." She picked up her backpack and hooked it over her shoulder.

A feminine cry of outrage startled them. "Everyone wants to be me! Everyone wants what Mac and I share!" The voice was high, strained and nasty, full of rage and pain.

Morgan stiffened and turned, afraid of what she'd see. Lila Markham's eyes were wild.

The blonde in the beige car. A shiver of recognition ran down her back. She darted a glance at Rory. He looked surprisingly calm.

"Out to the pool." Lila trained a small handgun at Morgan's midsection. Her makeup had smeared, her designer dress looked as if she'd worn it for days, and it seemed she hadn't used soap and water for just as long.

Dumbfounded, Morgan froze, her mind on a frenzied search for anything remotely familiar about the situation.

"You're the blonde who followed me in the beige car!" Bad time to blurt the obvious but her brain was working double time to process the scene. Lila's gun never wavered and Morgan finally focused on getting away from the little barrel.

"And you sent the photos," Rory stated calmly as if the images had been of a family vacation. He radiated an energy Lila was too wild to see. "Lila, sorry I didn't hear you come in. The ears, you know." He tapped the side of his head. "I'm glad you got past the horde at the gates."

He was up to something. She tried to catch his eye, but he stared at Lila, willing her to look at him.

If she did turn her attention to the old man, Morgan could jump her, grab the gun and—what? People in a state like this were superstrong, jacked up on adrenaline and rage. Morgan wouldn't stand a chance against her.

A cold shiver of fear trailed down her spine as she realized the futility of rushing the woman.

The phone rang in a loud trill by Rory's hand. He started, but then muted the ringer without answering. The call went to voice mail. "Lila, how did you get in?"

"I copied the key for the shed." She jerked her head to the French door, where a set of keys hung. "And for the pool house." Lila stood in the kitchen beside the island, one hand braced on the granite countertop. A tinier woman than she looked on movie screens, she kept her weapon on Morgan. If Morgan rushed her, she'd be framed in the doorway, a hard target to miss.

Lila's eyes snapped. "You were ridiculously easy to follow. I watched you leave the estate in that god-awful truck and I had my brother learn everything he could about you."

She waved the gun again. "I told you to go out to the pool."

"Why should we go to the pool?" Rory asked. "We're perfectly comfortable in here." His monotone sounded reasonable, as if a woman in his kitchen with a gun was an everyday situation.

Lila blinked as if to clear her head. She addressed Morgan in a stringent voice. "If you don't jump into the pool, I'll shoot Rory. I'll start with his right foot, then his left. How long can you bear his screams?"

Morgan's stomach twisted. She'd seen some off-the-wall behavior, but Lila's dead-calm face chilled her to the bone. She wasn't sure she could move if she needed to.

But Rory could. He sidled half his body in front of Morgan. "It's too cold for a swim, Lila," he said in a calm voice.

"She's not going to swim, she's going to drown."

Morgan eased back to give Rory room to maneuver toward the distraught actress. "Put that down," she said firmly. "I'm damn tired of guns." Ignoring the thing would not make it go away.

Lila moved closer, hatred glowing on her face. She held the delicate-looking gun with a steady hand. "I can't see why Kingston would choose to fuck a piece of trash when he had me." She slid her gaze from the top of Morgan's head to her toes. "Filthy whore."

"It's odd that you mention Kingston's habit with women," Rory broke in. "Morgan and I were discussing that very thing before you came in."

"What?" Confused and distracted, Lila turned from Morgan to Rory.

"Morgan was saying that she didn't want to stay long enough to be discarded. She understands that will happen. It's how Mr. McRae does things." Rory nodded sagely, as if they all agreed. "He teases a woman with promises, then moves on without a care. It's a failing of his. He should have understood you weren't like the others, Lila. You never were."

Rory not only knew a thing or two about picking locks, he was one smooth talker. Lila hung on every word, nodding in agreement. "Yes, that's right. But he didn't mean to do that to me."

"He was disappointed to hear of your engagement,

Lila." Rory nodded in time with Lila. She followed his lead, moving like a marionette. "He was about to call you when he got the news. That was a difficult morning, as you can imagine."

Lila gave Rory a vacant smile as if she were playing out a fantasy behind her eyes.

Morgan gasped at the lie. Rory was scary smooth. "Navy, my ass," she muttered. She cocked an eyebrow at him, then hefted her backpack to her shoulder. Following Rory's lead, she aimed for nonchalant. "I'm leaving, Ms. Markham. I'm aware of who I am, where I come from, and I don't have any fantasies of happily ever after with Kingston McRae."

Lila motioned with the gun for Morgan to move around her. Rory stilled, clearly hoping to split Lila's attention.

The door to the patio stood open, an escape offered. Ten steps to freedom.

Rory cleared his throat. "Best of luck, Ms. Swann. Lila, I was about to make tea. You always enjoyed my chamomile. Could I interest you in a cup?" He moved smoothly toward a cupboard while Morgan eased her way toward the open door. "I don't believe you've seen the completed renovation, have you?"

Seven steps.

"No." Lila followed him with her eyes, but kept the gun on Morgan. She waved Morgan toward the open door. "Get out. But leave your cell phone here."

Shocked, Morgan looked at her hand and saw that she still held her phone. Mac had called and she'd ignored it. Had he been trying to warn her that Lila had left? She dropped the phone to the floor with a clatter, her hand nerveless.

Three steps to freedom. Or death. Was Lila simply

waiting for her to clear the room then shoot? Would she kill Rory, too? Thoughts rolled one after the other, each more terrifying.

One step.

Morgan's breath stopped, her ears roared, her blood rushed.

From the corner of her eye she saw Rory reach into the cupboard while she stepped through the door onto the patio. Bracing for a bullet in the back, she shut her eyes and saw Mac's face. If she had to die, she wanted his to be the last face she saw. She squeezed her eyes tight and waited in a deathly silence.

"We'll have tea." Rory's calm voice drifted to Morgan's ears. "I'm parched," he said. "Tell me what you think of the renovations, Lila. Are they what you imagined? I took your advice to have a sink installed in the island."

Morgan took three more careful steps, holding her breath, waiting for Lila's response.

"The last time I was here, the kitchen was still a mess." Lila's voice had lost its edginess. "The room's lovely."

The incongruity of the small talk finally made Morgan understand she'd been dismissed. She dragged in a deep breath and bolted around the pool to hide behind the hot tub. From there she could watch the kitchen.

Rory took down a box of tea and went to get the kettle, his movements slow and methodical.

He looked fine, his hands steady, while Lila seemed animated and happy. She sat at the island, on the same stool where Morgan had watched Mac make the omelet. The tableau seemed surreal under the circumstances, but Morgan was sure Rory and Lila had played out the domestic scene many times before.

The only difference was the deadly piece of weaponry that lay on the counter within Lila's reach.

Hundreds of yards separated Morgan from the garden shed. Except for the huge maple tree, the expansive lawn provided very little cover. If she was quick, and Rory kept Lila's attention, she could make it to safety and find a phone.

But she couldn't leave Rory alone with a madwoman. One wrong word and he'd be killed.

In the distance, she heard sirens. Mac must have called the police after she'd shut off her phone and Rory had ignored the call on the landline. With a wry grin she realized the police showed up on Mercer Island a hell of a lot faster than they did anywhere else. But the sirens could frighten Lila. A frightened Lila was a dangerous Lila.

If the police screamed up that long driveway, the woman could slip over the edge into panic. Of course, Morgan hadn't thought to close the slider behind her. Now it stood open to the outside breezes and the wailing squad cars.

She might be less socially acceptable than Lila Markham, and had come from a less-than-perfect family. She would certainly be the next ex-bed partner of Kingston McRae, but Morgan Swann was no coward.

She ran back around the pool, keeping low and half hidden by the patio table and chairs where she and Mac had had lunch that first day.

By using the French door to the den, she could get inside without Lila seeing her from the kitchen.

She made a low, crouching dash for the door and slipped inside the house, grateful Rory had left the screen open and unlocked.

Brilliant. Now what? She was unarmed and Lila's lethal weapon sat within inches of her hand.

"What was that?" Lila said at the sound of the front door opening.

"Morgan! Rory! Lila wasn't at her hotel," Mac called from the foyer, agitated.

God! No! Not now. Mac would walk into a nightmare.

Morgan moved silently through the den. If Mac saw her, she might stave off disaster.

"Mac darling! We're in the kitchen having tea. Please join us!" The edginess was back in Lila's voice as she called out.

Mac would walk into a death trap if Morgan didn't do something. She eased along the wall to peek into the kitchen without exposing herself.

The scene was exactly the way she'd pictured it. Lila held her gun, but it wasn't aimed at Rory. It was aimed at the hall, just waiting for Mac to stride into range.

A familiar rush of adrenaline drowned out her hearing, but she screamed, "Mac! Lila's got a gun!"

Lila spun to face the den. Her eyes were glassy as she tightened her finger on the trigger. Morgan leaped out from behind the den wall and straight at the frightened, wild woman.

Rory moved faster and gave Lila's outstretched hand a chop on the wrist that sent the gun skidding along the island and off the edge. It landed with a heavy thud on the floor while Lila yelled in outrage and hugged her arm close to her chest.

Morgan heard nothing but the roar of her own pulse in her head. Her heart lurched in her chest as Mac barreled into the room.

She felt him at her back, hot and hard as he lifted and

swung her out of harm's way. She gasped for breath as her lungs kicked in and Rory and Jack swarmed Lila to restrain her.

Screams and threats filled the kitchen while Mac's strong arms cradled Morgan to his side.

"You scared the hell out of me!" His frustration couldn't hide his relief.

The thud of heavy feet sounded in the hall. The police.

Morgan released her breath and sagged into Mac's strength, letting him hold her as tightly as he wanted.

"Morgan, you could have been shot."

She couldn't tell which of them was shaking more. "I was afraid she'd shoot you. And I couldn't leave Rory here alone." She tore out of Mac's arms and checked on Rory, now seated and pale on a stool.

She patted his forearm and he clasped her hand, gave it a light squeeze. "Thank you, Morgan. You did a good job distracting her. When I heard Mac's voice I was too far away to reach her. She had the gun up and ready to fire before I could react."

"Adrenaline," she said. "Lila was jacked sky-high on it, ready to shoot anyone who stood in her way."

"Even Mac," Rory said.

"Even Mac."

"You need to give the kid a break," Morgan stated. They sat in the den, Morgan on the floor beside the big-screen television, facing the men. Jack glowered.

"Why?" Mac watched her with avid interest from his customary position by the window. The look sent heated shivers down her spine. He wanted her.

Alone.

He needed to bury himself in her and know they were

both alive and unharmed. She knew because she felt the same way. She wanted everyone to fade away so she could walk into Mac's arms and feel the pull of life.

But first, she had to plead her case for Jonathan Lake. "He's much younger than Lila, barely an adult. And he's spent his life a victim of his sister's unpredictable rages. He did what he could to protect himself while exposing her." She made sure to catch and hold each man's gaze in turn. They had to understand. "He's been bullied and emotionally scarred his whole life."

"You believe he left a cyber trail so we'd catch him?"

She nodded. "You said yourself he was smart. He tried to stop her by leading you to himself. He was probably waiting for the campus police, praying they'd get there before she did something violent. Can't you talk to the District Attorney? The police? Somebody?"

Jack's face turned grim. "You caught a break from a judge, so he deserves one?"

She nodded and looked at Mac.

"You wouldn't be the woman you are without having had that time in the halfway house," he said. "Your life might have gone differently if you'd been exposed to hard-core felons in jail."

"He's no criminal, nor is he sick like Lila." She could only imagine what it took for him to defy his sister.

Mac shook his head, but his eyes blazed guilty pain. "Lila told me she wanted more. She was ready to settle down, to marry. She wanted someone who wasn't involved in the movie business. I fit the bill, but there was no one I wanted less than Lila Markham. By the time she understood that, her career was disintegrating. I had no idea she'd been on medication for years. My rejecting her tipped her over the edge and she stopped taking the drugs she needs."

"Has she been violent in the past?" Jack asked.

He nodded. "I've had a long talk with her father. He's devastated by Jonathan's involvement." He crossed the den to sit in the lounger Rory had used earlier. "For years, before her family got help for her, she exploded into rages. Jonathan took the brunt. The parents couldn't leave him alone with her."

"He must have been terrified." Morgan's heart throbbed for the boy.

"That's why he left the cyber trail that led my IT team to him," Jack said with a nod. "If he hadn't made it so complicated we'd have got there sooner."

Mac continued. "He wanted to turn her in before she did anyone harm, but he couldn't be up-front about it. He's still afraid of her and doesn't want her to know he betrayed her. He hoped to trick her into thinking it was good detective work that stopped her, not that he'd let himself be found."

"Do you have to press charges?" Morgan asked.

"The police will. I'll see to it Lila gets the help she needs. The family's already been to a lawyer. Seems the brother told his parents only last night that she was dangerous again. They'll do everything they can for her."

"What about Jonathan?"

Jack glanced at Mac. "I'll explain it would have taken longer to find them if it weren't for what he did."

"Be careful there, Jack. Someone might think you're a nice guy under all that stern dedication to duty." Morgan let a smile dance across her mouth for the first time today.

"Excuse us, Jack, but that smile is the only thing I've wanted to see all day. So get out."

The minute the front door closed behind him, Morgan launched herself at Mac and let him sweep her into his arms. "I want to take you somewhere," he said between hungry kisses.

"This won't involve a passport, will it?"

He took her by the hand. "Run," he said.

He tugged and she followed, giddy to finally be alone.

HELICOPTERS FLEW OVERHEAD and the gates swarmed with photographers. Mac didn't care. No one would see them.

He disabled the motion sensor lights in the garage as she waited breathlessly beside the Morgan.

Mac wanted the dark so she couldn't see the stark terror he still felt.

Her courageous leap at Lila still burned his retinas. He opened the car's back door.

"Oh, Mr. McRae, you don't mean to steam up the windows, do you?"

"Every chance I get."

Morgan thrilled at the spicy invitation. "But this is Lindsay's car. Are you sure you want to—"

"I'll buy her another one. Now get in."

She climbed into the backseat and scooted to the far side. "You're a vision in this car, my Morgan." He followed her inside.

Her small hand cupped his cheek and drew his face close to hers. "Your Morgan? Do you mean the car?"

"You know what I mean." The flare in her eyes told him she did. He leaned into the promise she offered.

"Kiss me, Mac, and get my heart back to beating. I think it stopped in the kitchen."

"Mine, too. Especially when I saw you leap out at

Lila." He blinked away the sudden vision and the fear that came with it.

She clicked her tongue. "Adrenaline and fear. It's a scary combination. Makes you do wild things."

"Don't leave, Morgan. I don't want you to go."

She patted his cheek. "I'll like Miami. It'll be a fresh start. I've done it before, I can do it again." She blinked back a sheen in her eyes. "Don't worry about me."

"Miami? You're running off to Miami?"

"My mom lives there with Ernie."

"Husband number?"

"Seven, but this time it's the real thing. Even Elizabeth Swann gets a happy ending."

"So do we."

Suspicion burrowed into the glow in her eyes. "Why?"

"I've got a house near Miami. I'd like to take you there."

She looked doubtful. "Mac, do you think that's wise?"

"We need time to explore each other." He was sure of his feelings, but she had him in knots about hers. "We can visit Elizabeth and Ernie, walk the beach, make love." He tucked a wave of lustrous hair behind her ear. "Make more love."

"I don't want my mother to get ideas about you and me. That'll be a pressure neither of us wants. Now that it looks like her wedding days are behind her, she may get it into her head to plan one for me."

He bit back the first thing that popped into his head. "We'll let her know we're taking it slow."

She looked even more suspicious. "Slow? You think this week's been slow?"

"We've packed a lifetime into a few days."

"We have." She gave him a solemn nod.

"Give us a chance, Morgan."

"Oh, Mac, don't ask me to stay unless you feel the way I do."

"How is that, Morgan? How do you feel?" His heart hammered and he felt a glimmer of hope.

"I love the man you are, the way you think, the way you make me laugh. I love the way you take responsibility and don't blame anyone else for your mistakes." She opened her eyes, tears filling them. "But I can't be with you if I'm just a public romance. Don't ask me to do that."

"What I want with you, Morgan Swann, is very, very private." He drew her onto his lap. "I love that you say what you think when you think it. I love that you're so strong and brave. Rory told me what you said to Lila about me moving on and how you were leaving before I could."

"Self-preservation. I am my mother's daughter, Mac. We don't stick around waiting to be dumped." She wriggled in his lap and made his blood rush south.

"I've treated a lot of women shabbily, Morgan. All those women on my arm in front of the cameras—none of that was real."

"Being seen with you helped their careers, too." She nibbled her lower lip.

"What I mean to say is, my father wasn't faithful, didn't know the meaning of the word. I can see how you might think the same thing of me. But believe me, when I make promises, I keep them."

"The way you promised to help Lindsay, and now Jonathan, too, and even Lila."

"I will." He kissed the tip of her nose. "You were so brave last night when that maniac shot at you and again today with Lila. Can you be brave enough to take a chance on me? On us. If you can handle what the tabloids dish out for the next few weeks, we can move on with our lives. Together." He waited, watched while tough-as-nails, sweet-as-candy Morgan Swann weighed his words.

How he loved her. Loved everything about her from her lustrous head of auburn waves to the tips of her sexy toes. Her pride impressed him. Her courage humbled him.

Drove him nuts, of course, but humbled him. "I've lived through what happens when the tabloids shred your life. I don't want to go through that again unless I have you waiting on the other side. We'll have new lives together."

"Together." She nodded. "I love you, Mac."

"I love you, Morgan." He kissed her hard and deep, her breasts flattening against his chest while she settled her softness on his hard length.

He slid his fingers up the back of her thighs and cradled her butt under her shorts. "You make me crazy."

"Good. Elizabeth says to keep 'em guessing."

"All that talk about what I love about you?"

She cast him a wary glance. "What about it?"

"You've got to know I hate your job. I won't ask you to quit, but please, think hard about something safer."

"And give up all the excitement?"

"We'll make enough of our own to last a lifetime."

"A lifetime," she echoed.

Harlequin offers a romance for every mood!
See below for a sneak peek
from our paranormal romance line,
Silhouette® Nocturne™.
Enjoy a preview of REUNION by USA TODAY
bestselling author Lindsay McKenna.

Aella closed her eyes and sensed a distinct shift, like movement from the world around her to the unseen world.

She opened her eyes. And had a slight shock at the man standing ten feet away. He wasn't just any man. Her heart leaped and pounded. He reminded her of a fierce warrior from an ancient civilization. Incan? She wasn't sure but she felt his deep power and masculinity.

I'm Aella. Are you the guardian of this sacred site? she asked, hoping her telepathy was strong.

Fox's entire body soared with joy. Fox struggled to put his personal pleasure aside.

Greetings, Aella. I'm the assistant guardian to this sacred area. You may call me Fox. How can I be of service to you, Aella? he asked.

I'm searching for a green sphere. A legend says that the Emperor Pachacuti had seven emerald spheres created for the Emerald Key necklace. He had seven of his priestesses and priests travel the world to hide these spheres from evil forces. It is said that when all seven spheres are found, restrung and worn, that Light will return to the Earth. The fourth sphere is here, at your sacred site. Are you aware of it? Aella held her breath. She loved looking at him, especially his sensual mouth. The desire to kiss him came out of nowhere.

Fox was stunned by the request. *I know of the Emerald Key necklace because I served the emperor at the time it was created. However, I did not realize that one of the spheres is here.*

Aella felt sad. Why? Every time she looked at Fox, her heart felt as if it would tear out of her chest. *May I stay in touch with you as I work with this site?* she asked.

Of course. Fox wanted nothing more than to be here with her. To absorb her ephemeral beauty and hear her speak once more.

Aella's spirit lifted. What *was* this strange connection between them? Her curiosity was strong, but she had more pressing matters. In the next few days, Aella knew her life would change forever. How, she had no idea….

Look for REUNION
By USA TODAY bestselling author
Lindsay McKenna
Available April 2010
Only from Silhouette® Nocturne™

OLIVIA GATES

BILLIONAIRE, M.D.

Dr. Rodrigo Valderrama has it all…
everything but the woman he's secretly
desired and despised. A woman forbidden
to him—his brother's widow.
And she's pregnant.

Cybele was injured in a plane crash
and lost her memory. All she knows is
she's falling for the doctor who has swept her
away to his estate to heal. If only the secrets
in his eyes didn't promise to tear
them forever apart.

Available March wherever you buy books.

Always Powerful, Passionate and Provocative.

Visit Silhouette Books at www.eHarlequin.com

SD73018

HARLEQUIN®

INTRIGUE®

WILL THIS REUNITED FAMILY
BE STRONG ENOUGH TO EXPOSE
A LURKING KILLER?

FIND OUT IN THIS ALL-NEW
THRILLING TRILOGY FROM TOP
HARLEQUIN INTRIGUE AUTHOR

B.J. DANIELS

WHITEHORSE
MONTANA

Winchester Ranch

GUN-SHY BRIDE—*April 2010*

HITCHED—*May 2010*

TWELVE-GAUGE GUARDIAN—
June 2010

REQUEST YOUR FREE BOOKS!

2 FREE NOVELS PLUS 2 FREE GIFTS!

HARLEQUIN®

Blaze™

Red-hot reads!

HB10

COMING NEXT MONTH

Available March 30, 2010

www.eHarlequin.com